## DATE DUE

| | | | |
|---|---|---|---|
| | | | |
| | | | |
| | | | |
| | | | |
| | | | |
| | | | |
| | | | |
| | | | |
| | | | |
| | | | |
| | | | |
| | | | |
| | | | |

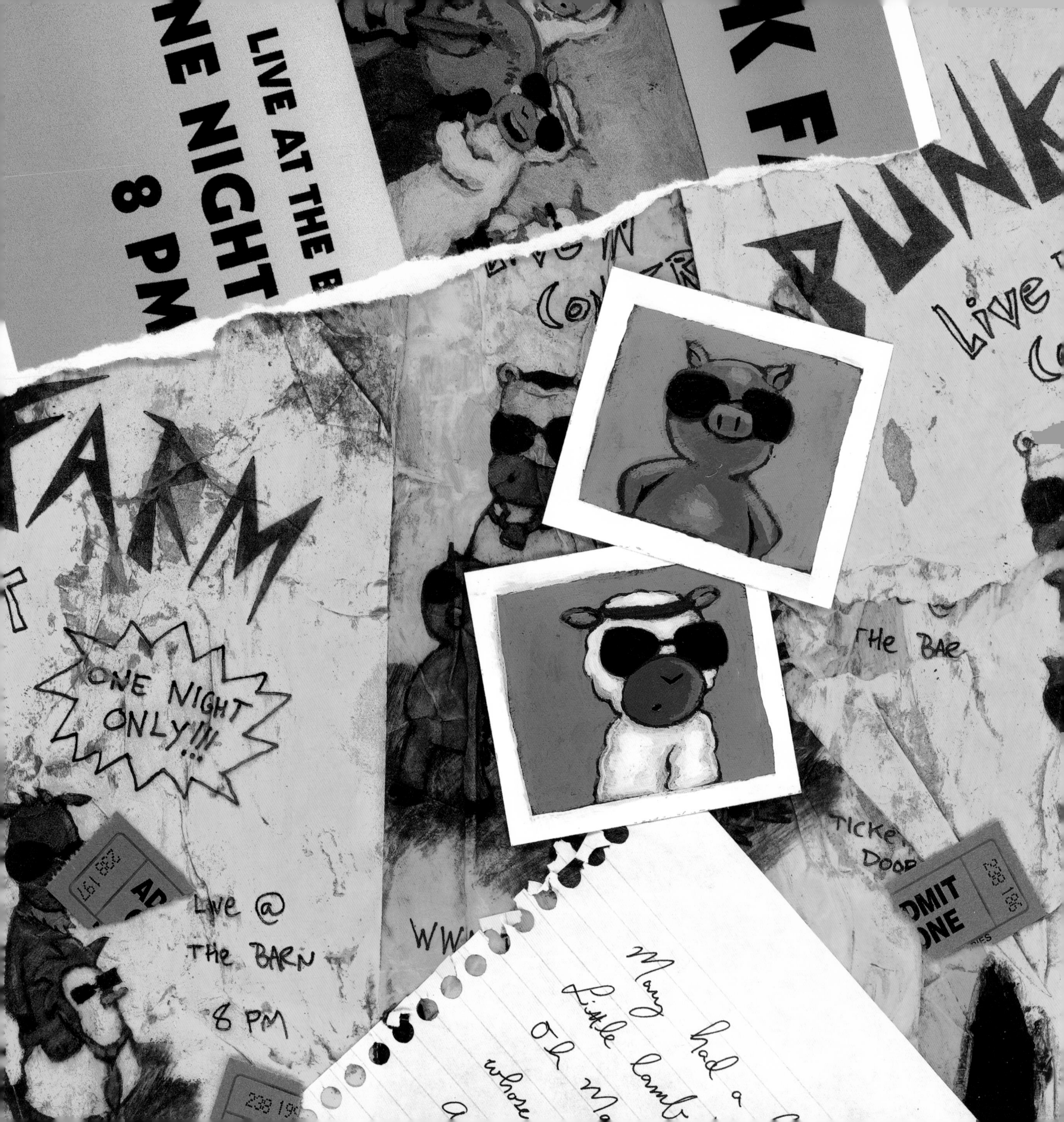

LIVE AT THE B
NE NIGHT
8 PM
K F
PUNK
Live T
FARM
ONE NIGHT ONLY!!!
Live @
The BARN
8 PM
THE BAR
TICKE
DOOR
ADMIT ONE
Mary had a
Little lamb
Oh Ma
whose

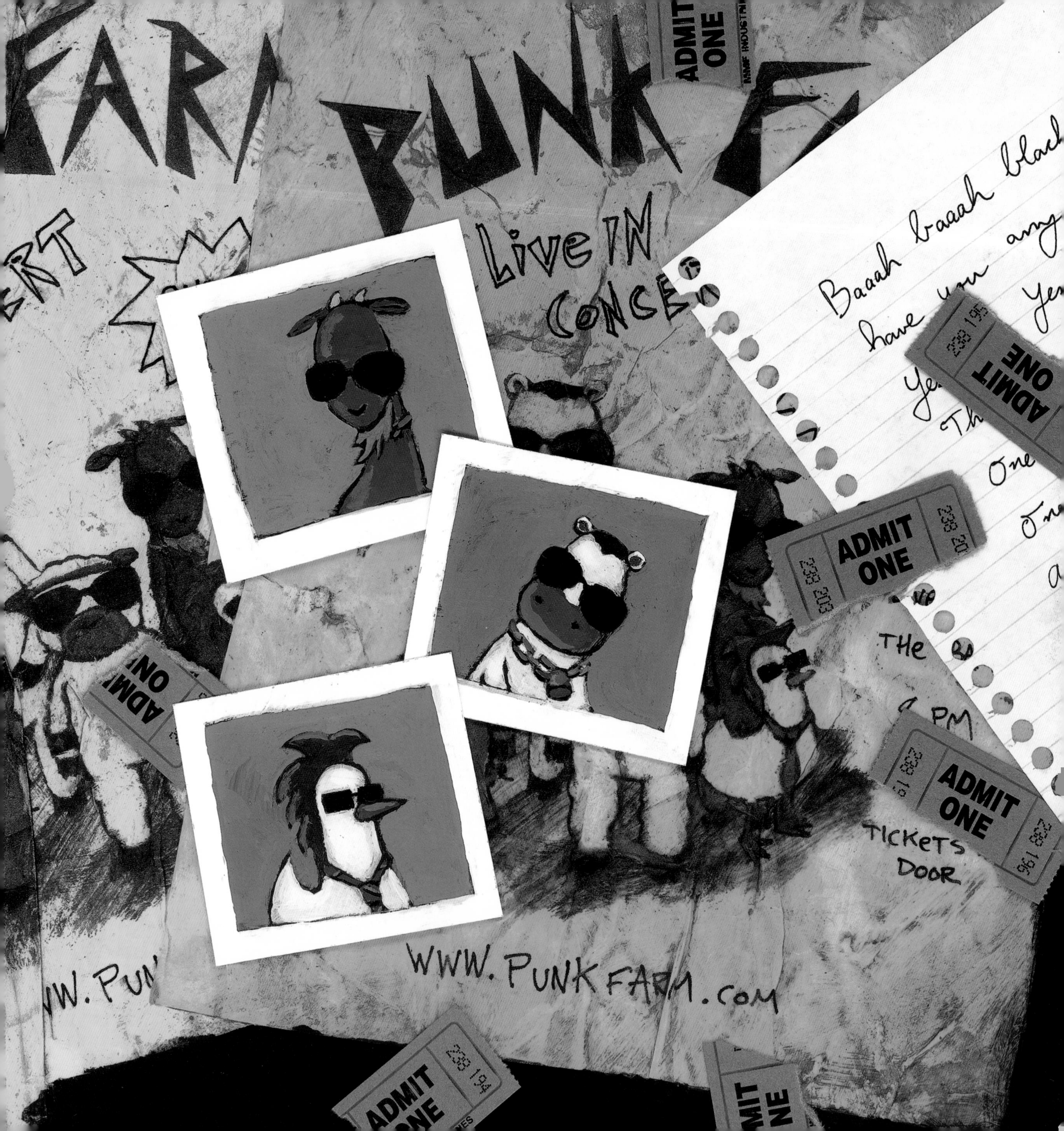

FARM
PUNK
ERT
LIVE IN
CONCE
ADMIT ONE
Baaah baaah black
have you any
ADMIT ONE
ADMIT ONE
ADMIT ONE
THE
PM
ADMIT ONE
TICKETS
DOOR
WWW.PUN
WWW.PUNKFARM.COM
ADMIT ONE
ADMIT ONE

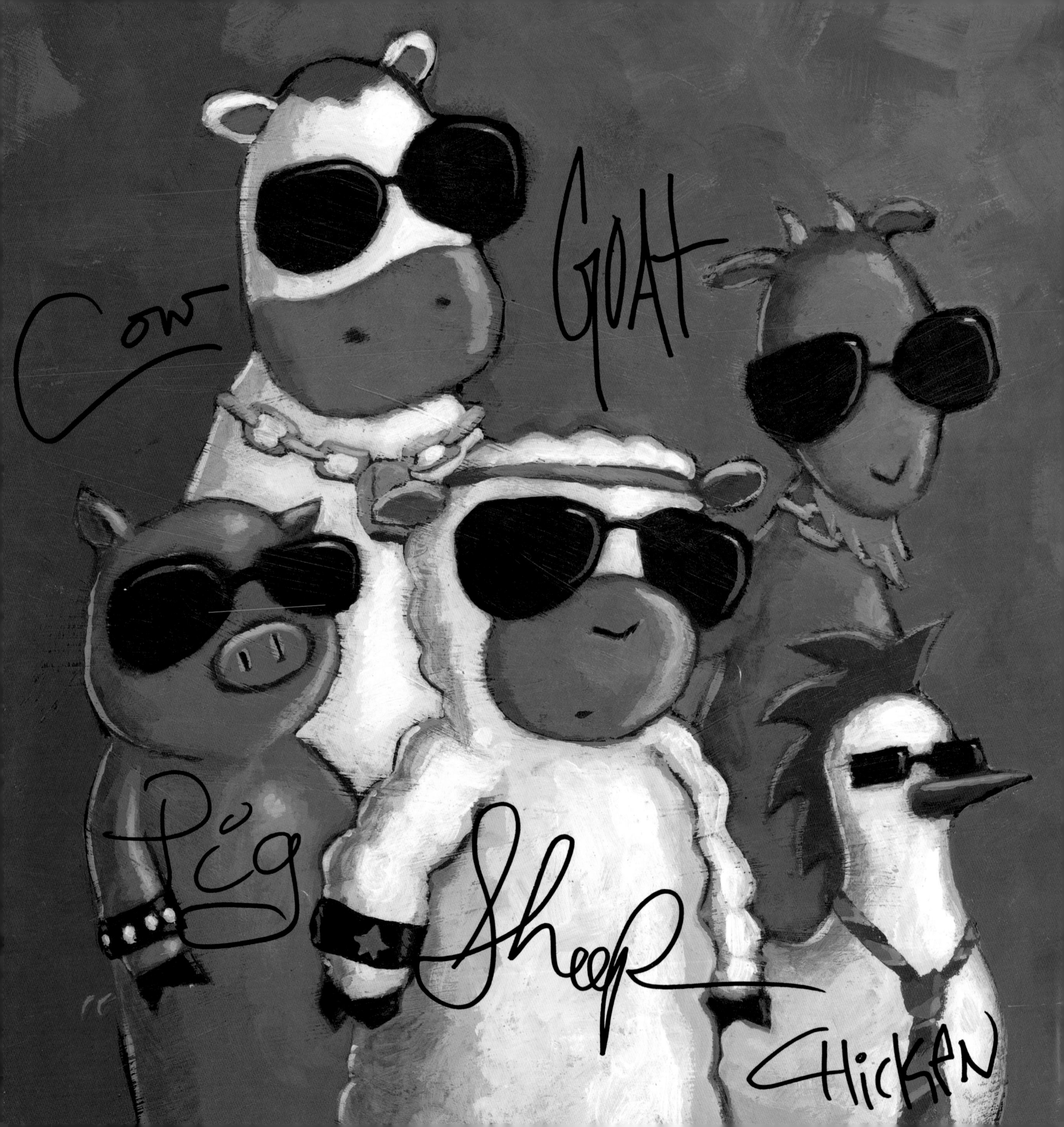
Cow
GOAT
Pig
Sheep
CHICKEN

# PUNK FARM

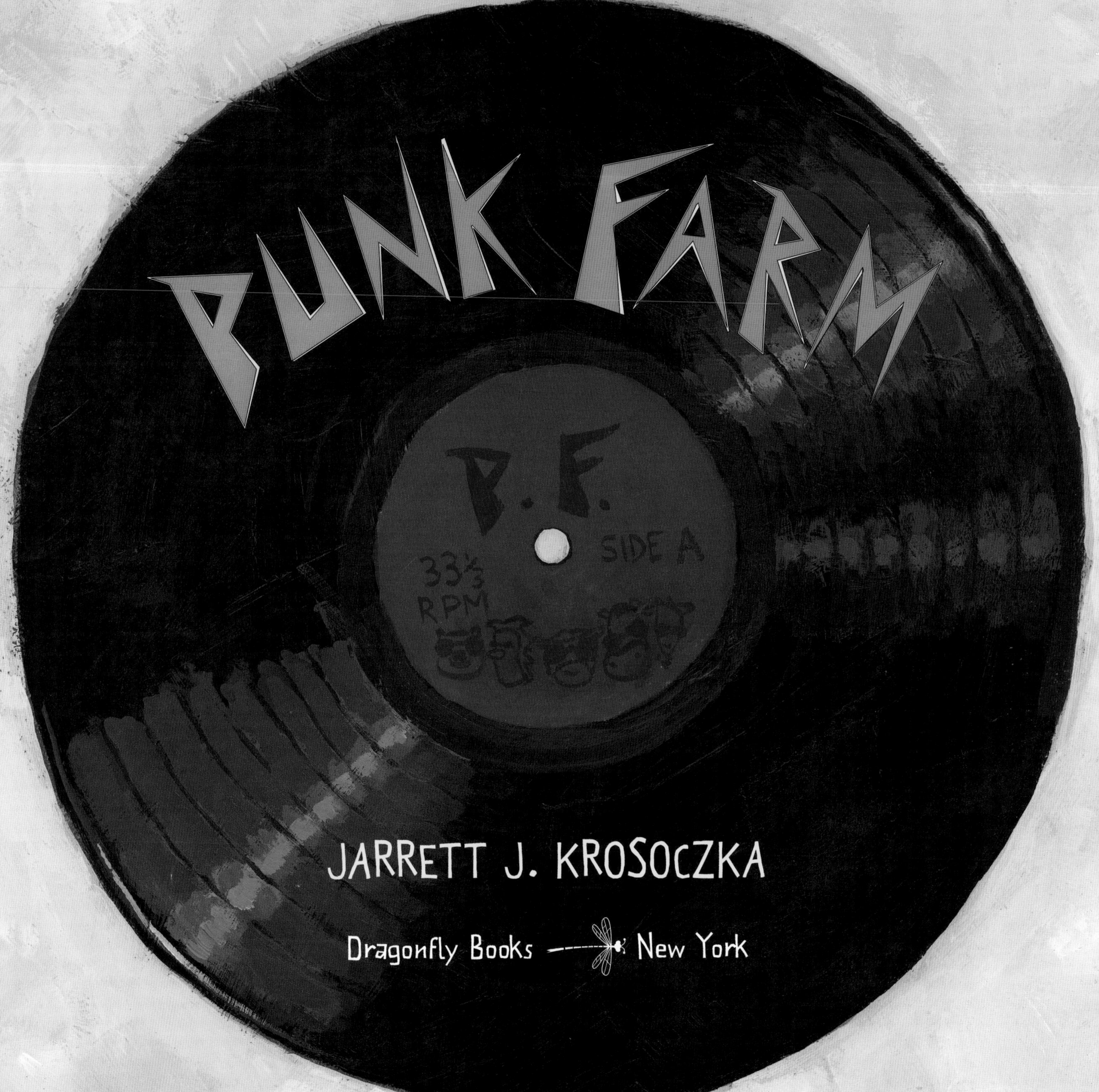
P.F.
SIDE A
33⅓ RPM

JARRETT J. KROSOCZKA

Dragonfly Books — New York

All rights reserved. Published in the United States by Dragonfly Books, an imprint of Random House Children's Books,
a division of Random House, Inc., New York. Originally published in hardcover in the United States by Alfred A. Knopf,
an imprint of Random House Children's Books, a division of Random House, Inc., New York, in 2005.

Dragonfly Books with the colophon is a registered trademark of Random House, Inc.

Visit us on the Web! www.randomhouse.com/kids

Educators and librarians, for a variety of teaching tools, visit us at
www.randomhouse.com/teachers

The Library of Congress has cataloged the hardcover edition of this work as follows:
Krosoczka, Jarrett.
Punk Farm / Jarrett J. Krosoczka.
p.   cm.
Summary: At the end of the day, while Farmer Joe gets ready for bed, his animals tune their instruments
to perform in a big concert as a rock band called Punk Farm.
ISBN 978-0-375-82429-6 (trade) — ISBN 978-0-375-92429-3 (lib. bdg.)
[1. Musicians–Fiction. 2. Rock music–Fiction. 3. Domestic animals–Fiction. 4. Farm life–Fiction.] I. Title.
PZ7.K935Pu 2005
[E]–dc22
2004018803

ISBN 978-0-440-41793-4 (pbk.)

MANUFACTURED IN CHINA

10 9 8 7 6 5 4 3
First Dragonfly Books Edition

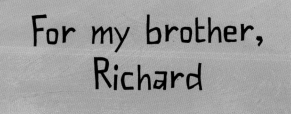

For my brother,
Richard

Farmer Joe works hard all day long.

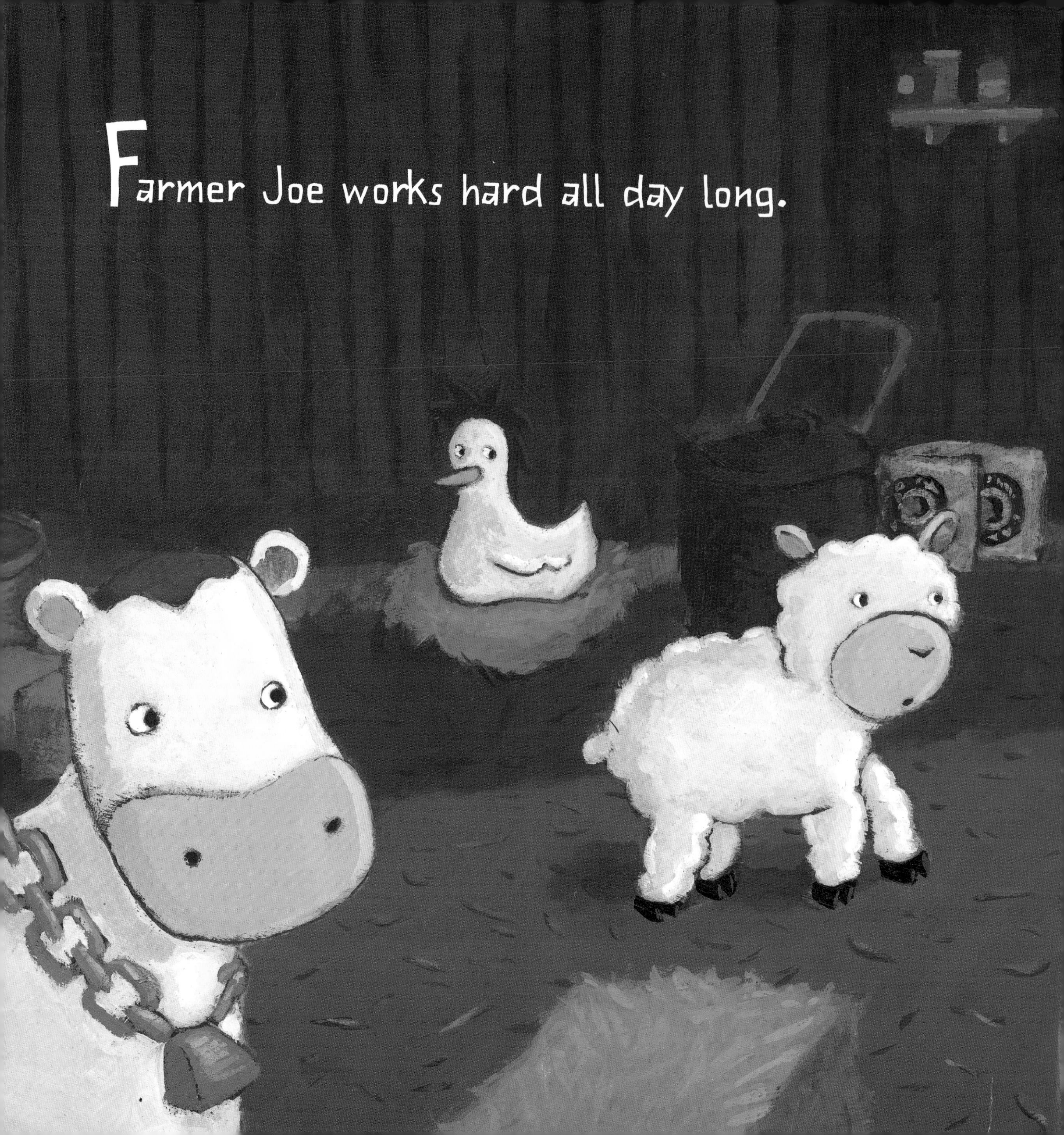

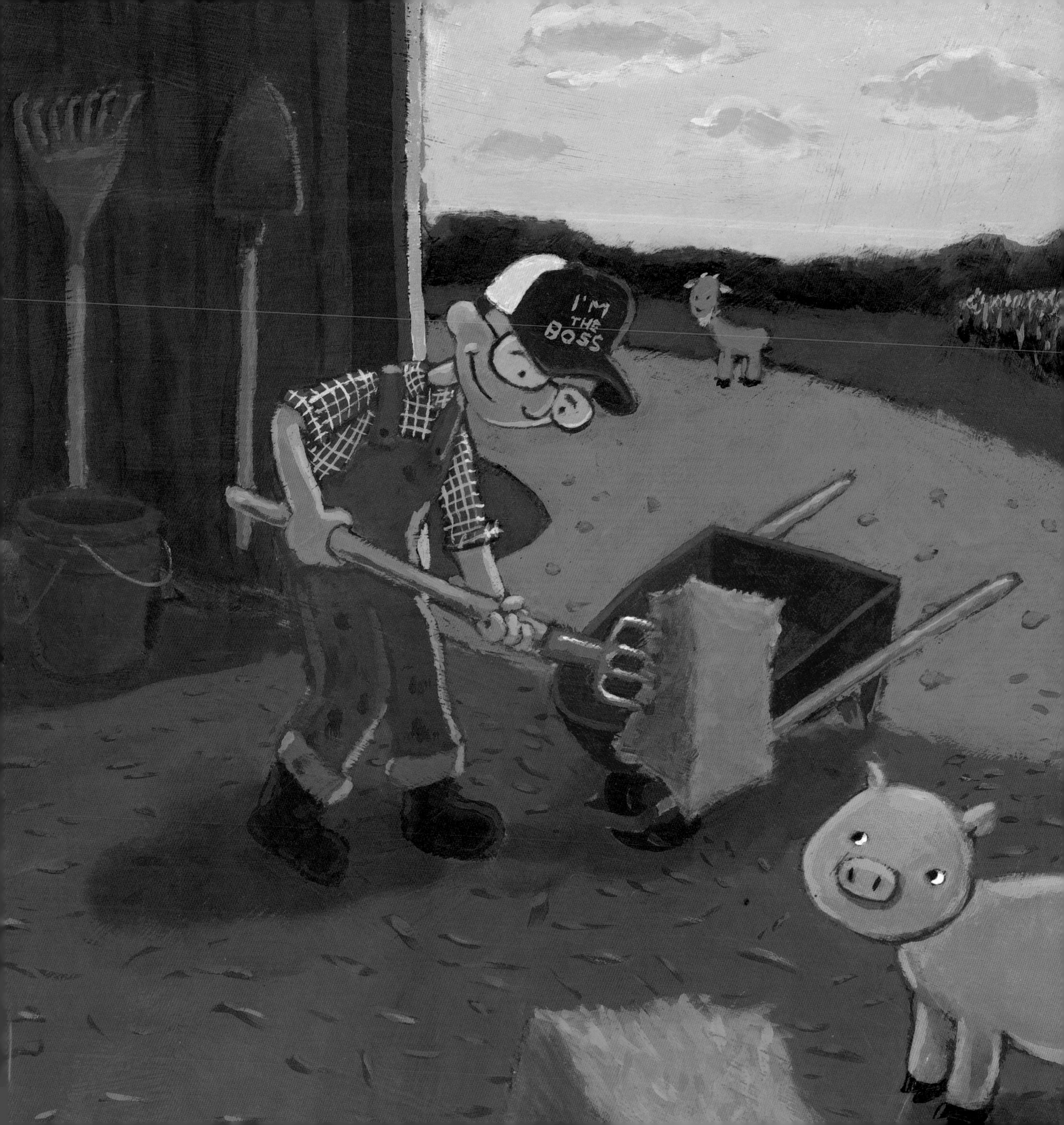
I'M
THE
BOSS

At the end of the day, Farmer Joe
is tired and heads home for bed.

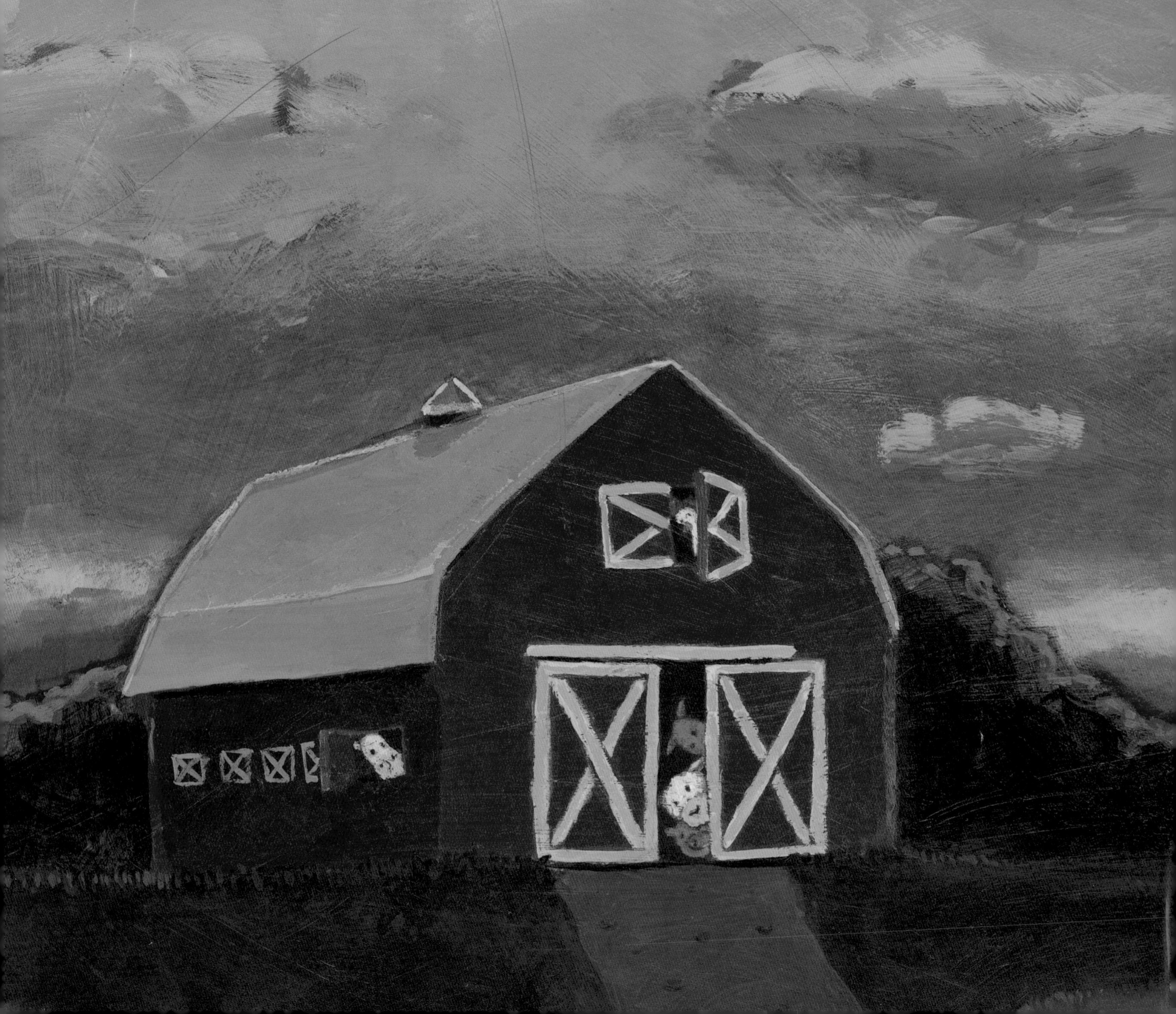

Farmer Joe's animals are sleepy, too.
But are they getting ready for bed?

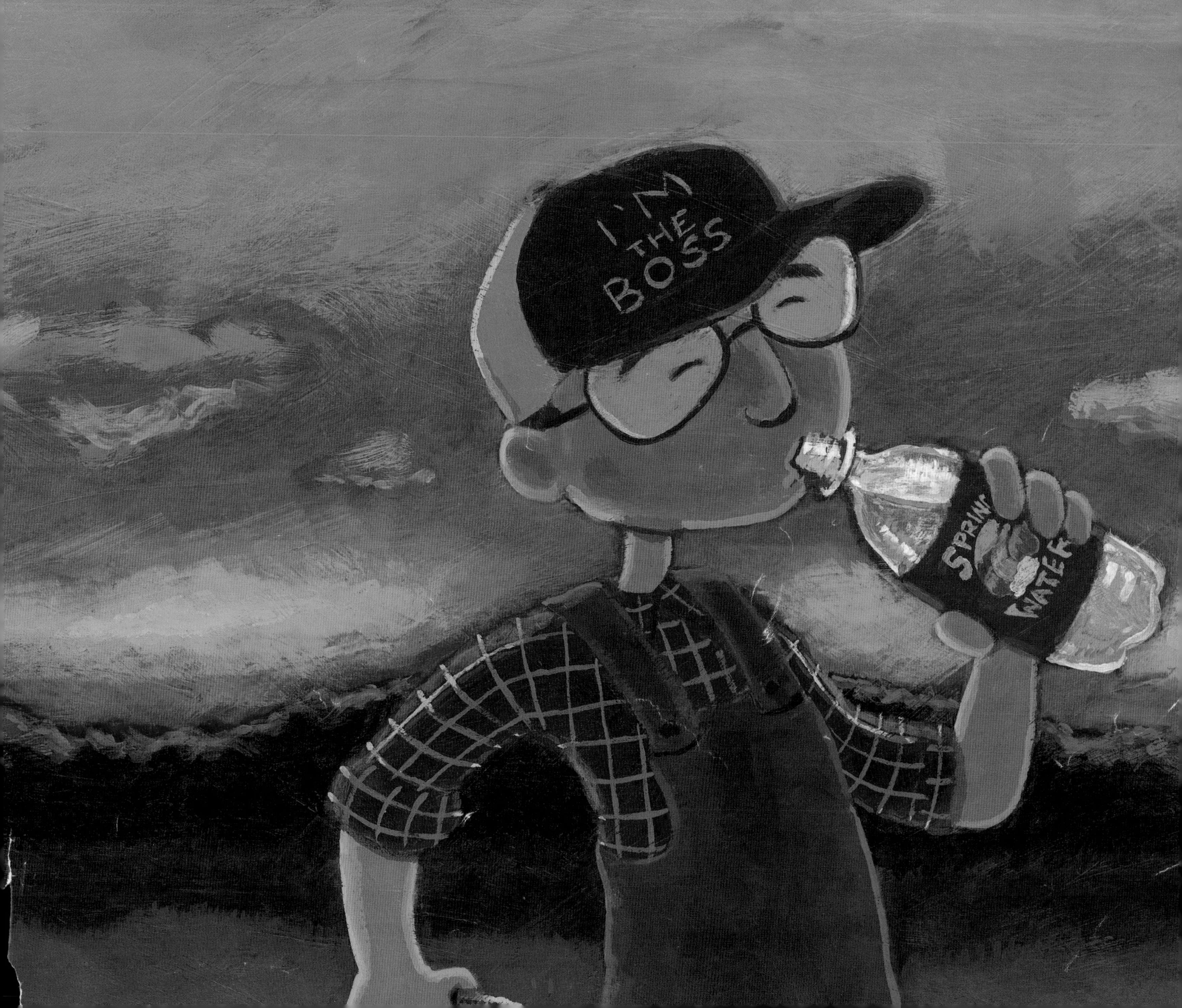
I'M THE BOSS
SPRING WATER

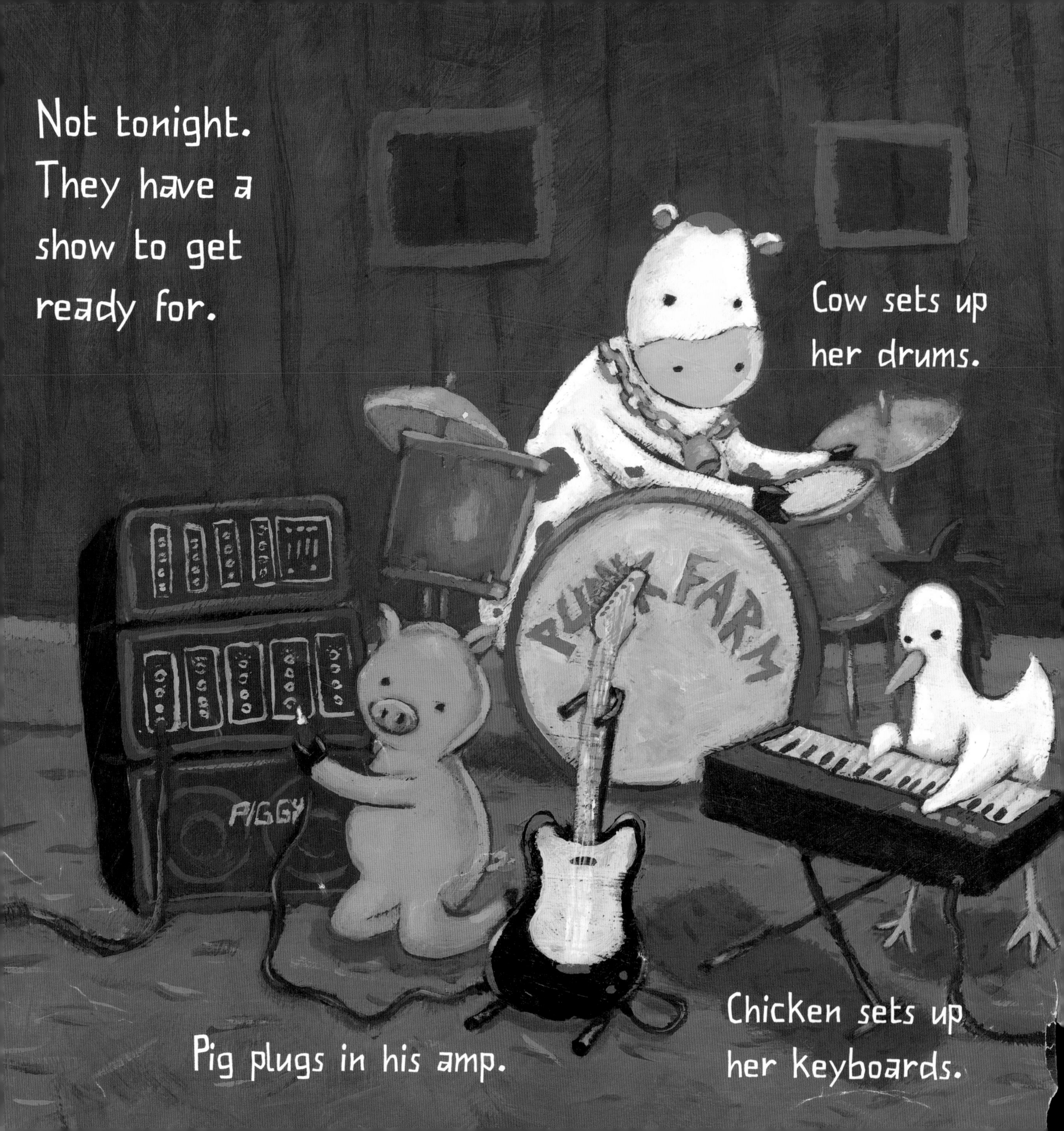
PIGGY

Not tonight. They have a show to get ready for.

Cow sets up her drums.

Pig plugs in his amp.

Chicken sets up her keyboards.

Sheep checks the microphone.
"Testing . . . 1 . . . 2 . . .
3 . . ."

Goat tunes his bass.

"Okay, gang, tonight's the big night! Let's go over some songs before this place gets packed!"

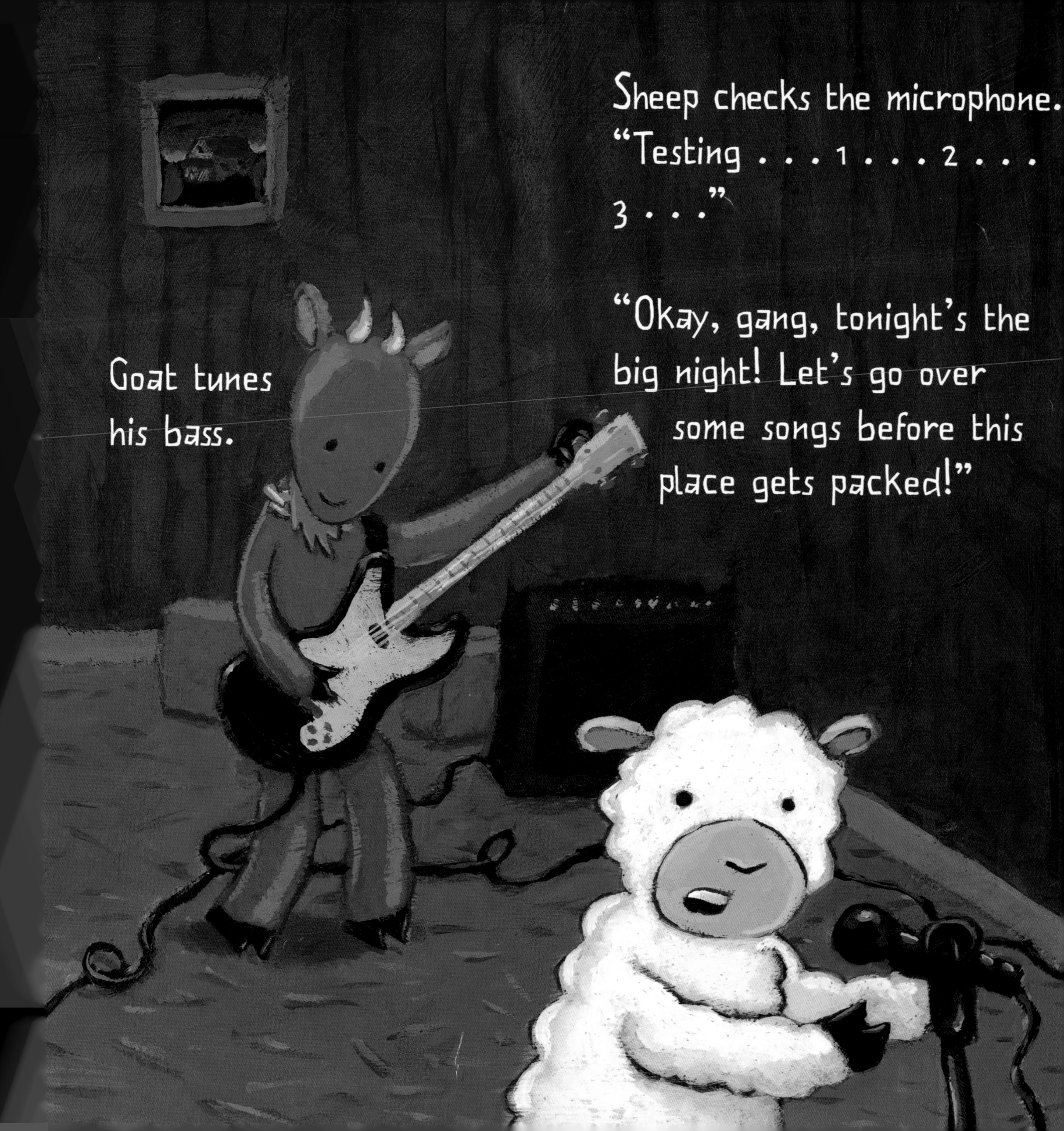

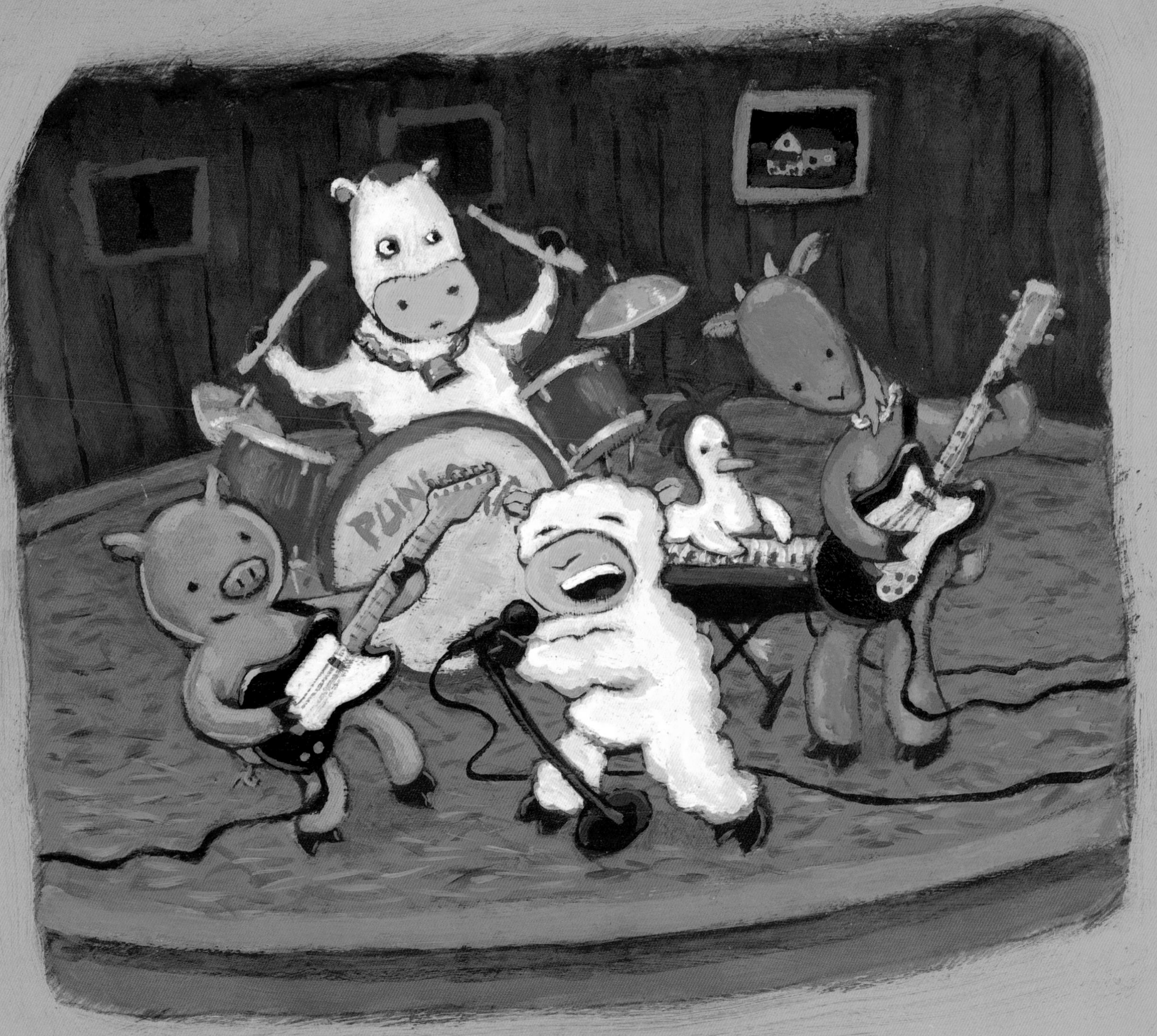

In the middle of practice, Cow stops drumming.
"Uh . . . guys!" she says. "The farmer's light is on!"

The animals freeze. The microphone screeches.
Footsteps can be heard in the distance.
Will they get caught?

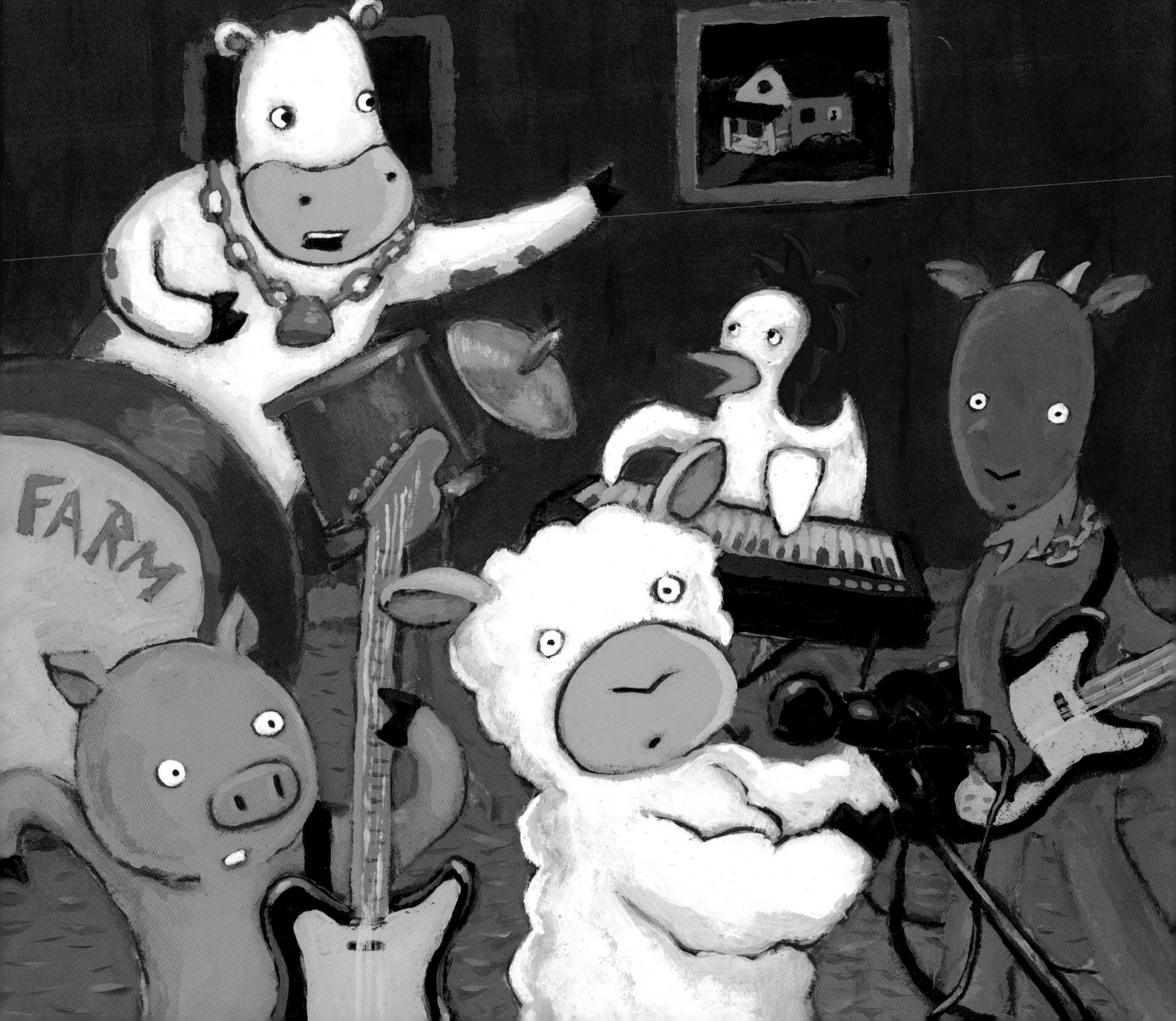
FARM

Not tonight. The light goes off, and Punk Farm finishes their rehearsal.

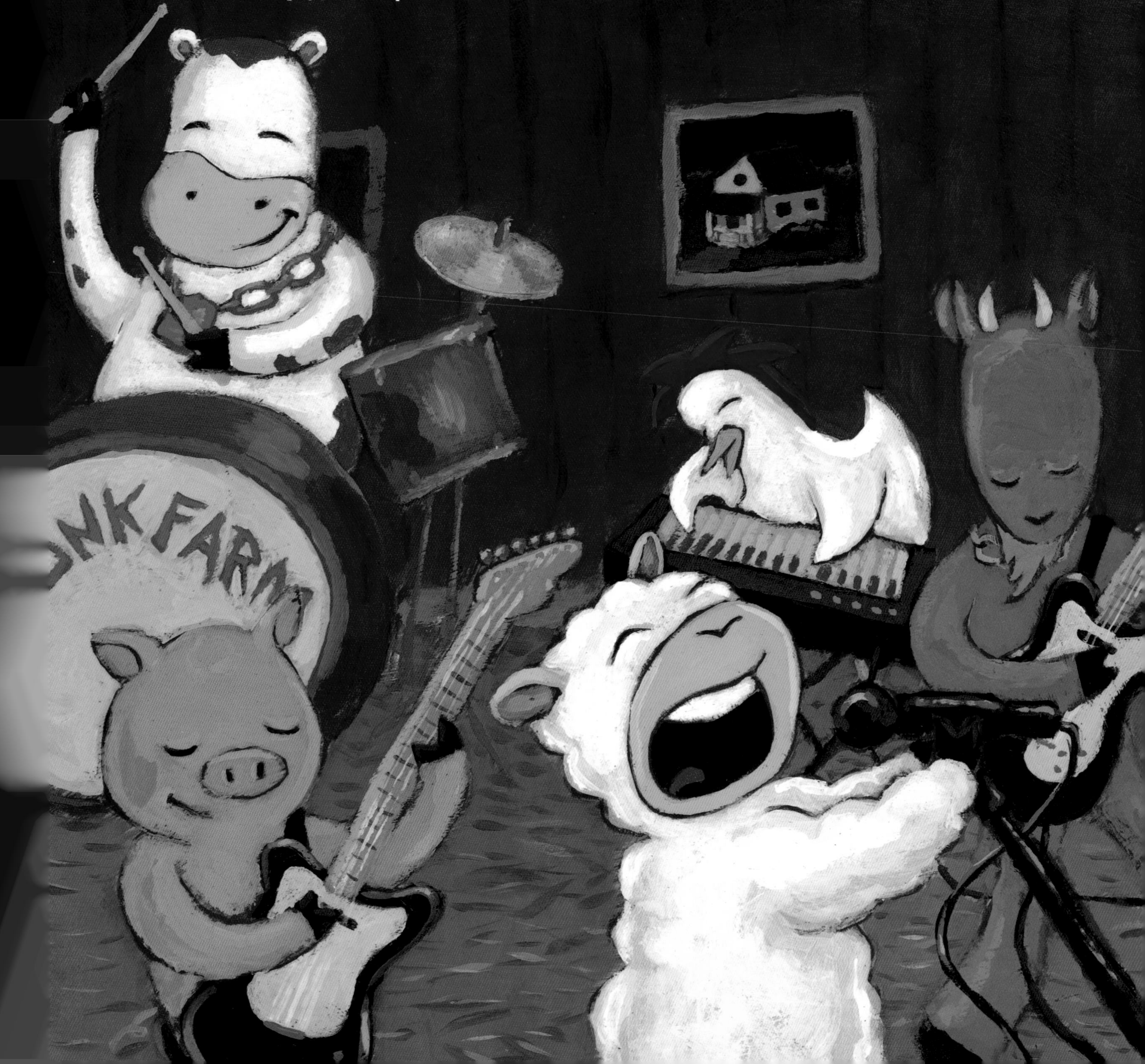

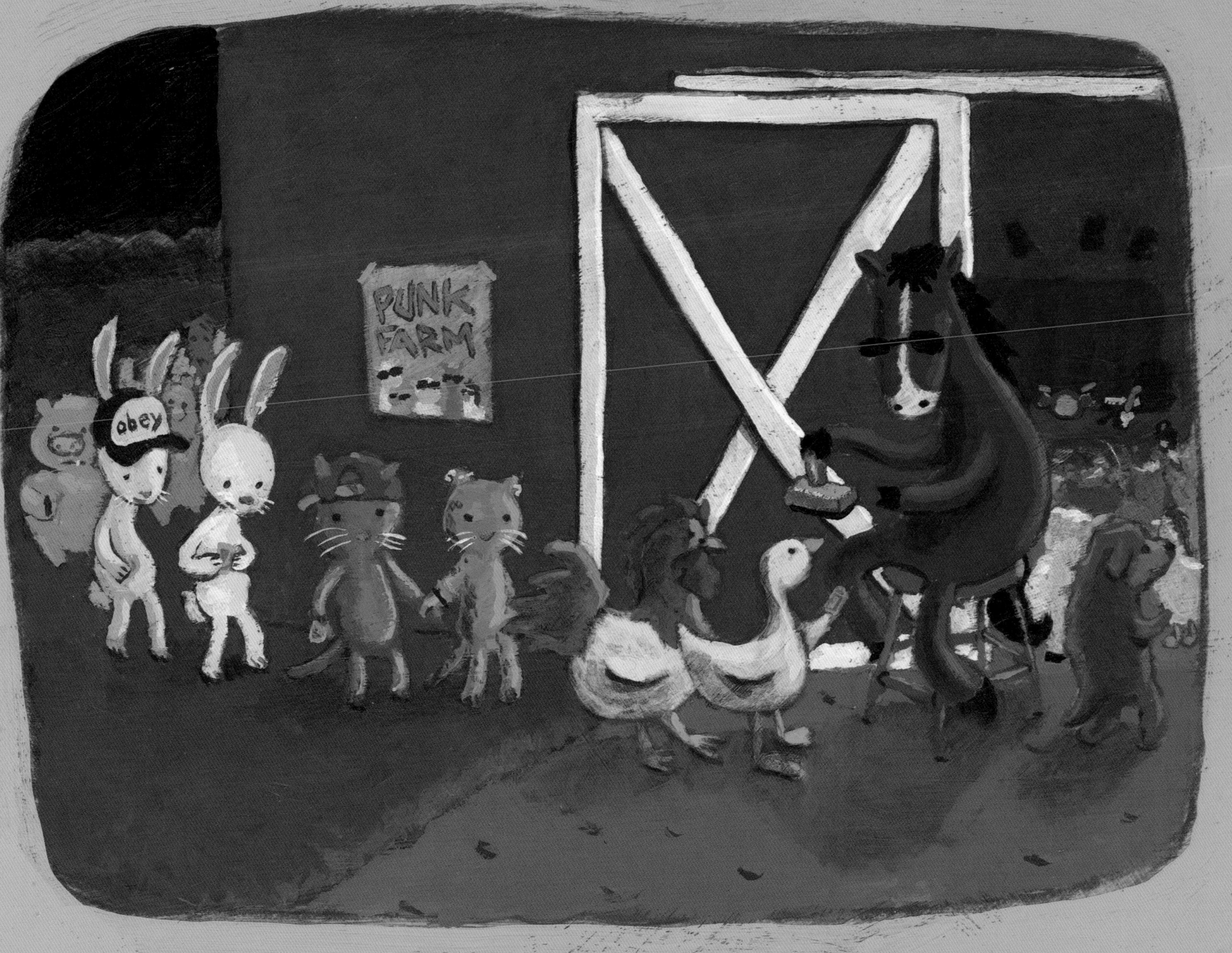
PUNK
FARM
obey

Outside, animals wait in line and buy tickets.
Everyone is eager for the show to start.

"Are you guys ready?" asks Sheep.
"I was born ready," says Pig.
"Whatever, dude," says Goat.

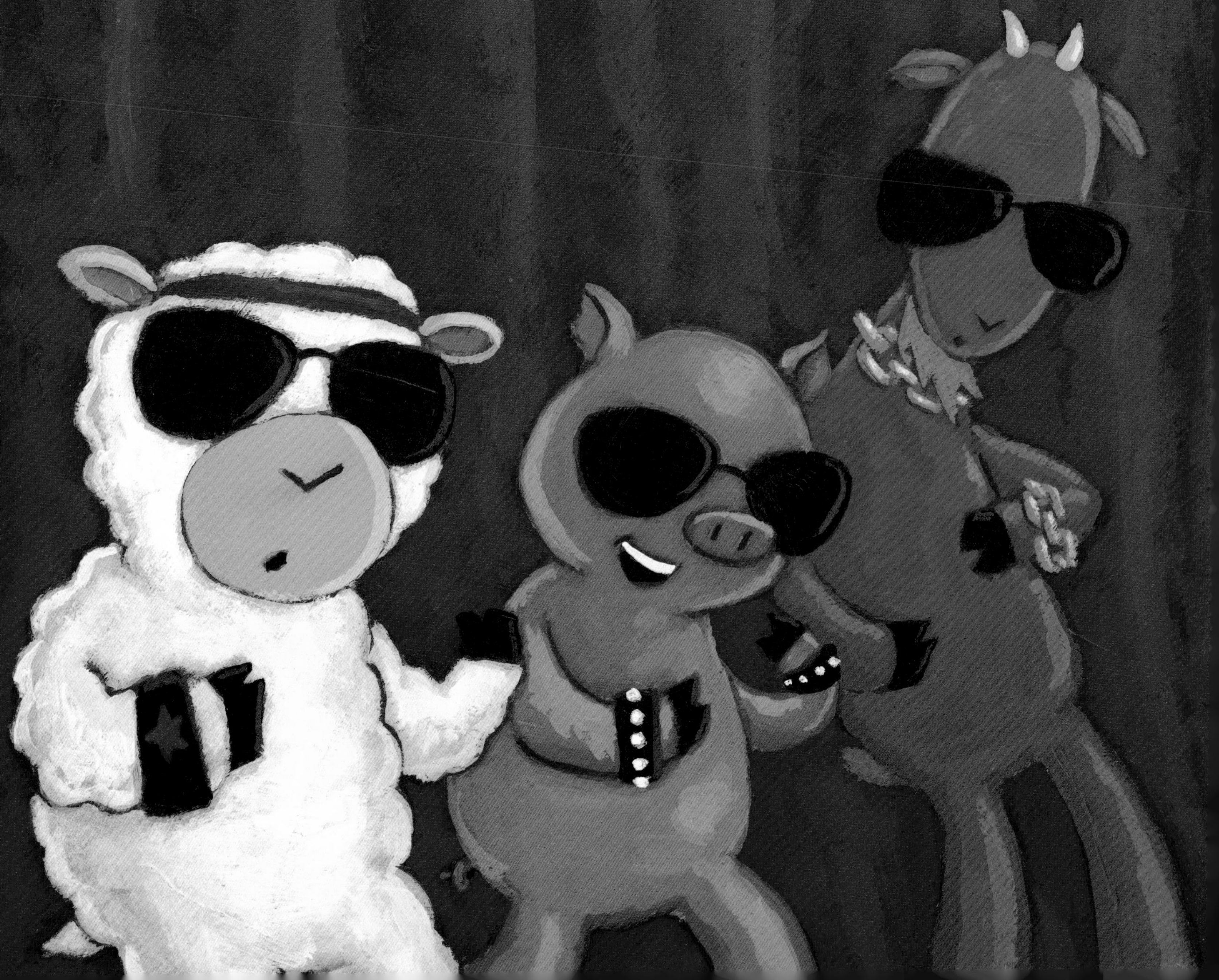

"I'm nervous," says Chicken.
"Let's do this!" says Cow.

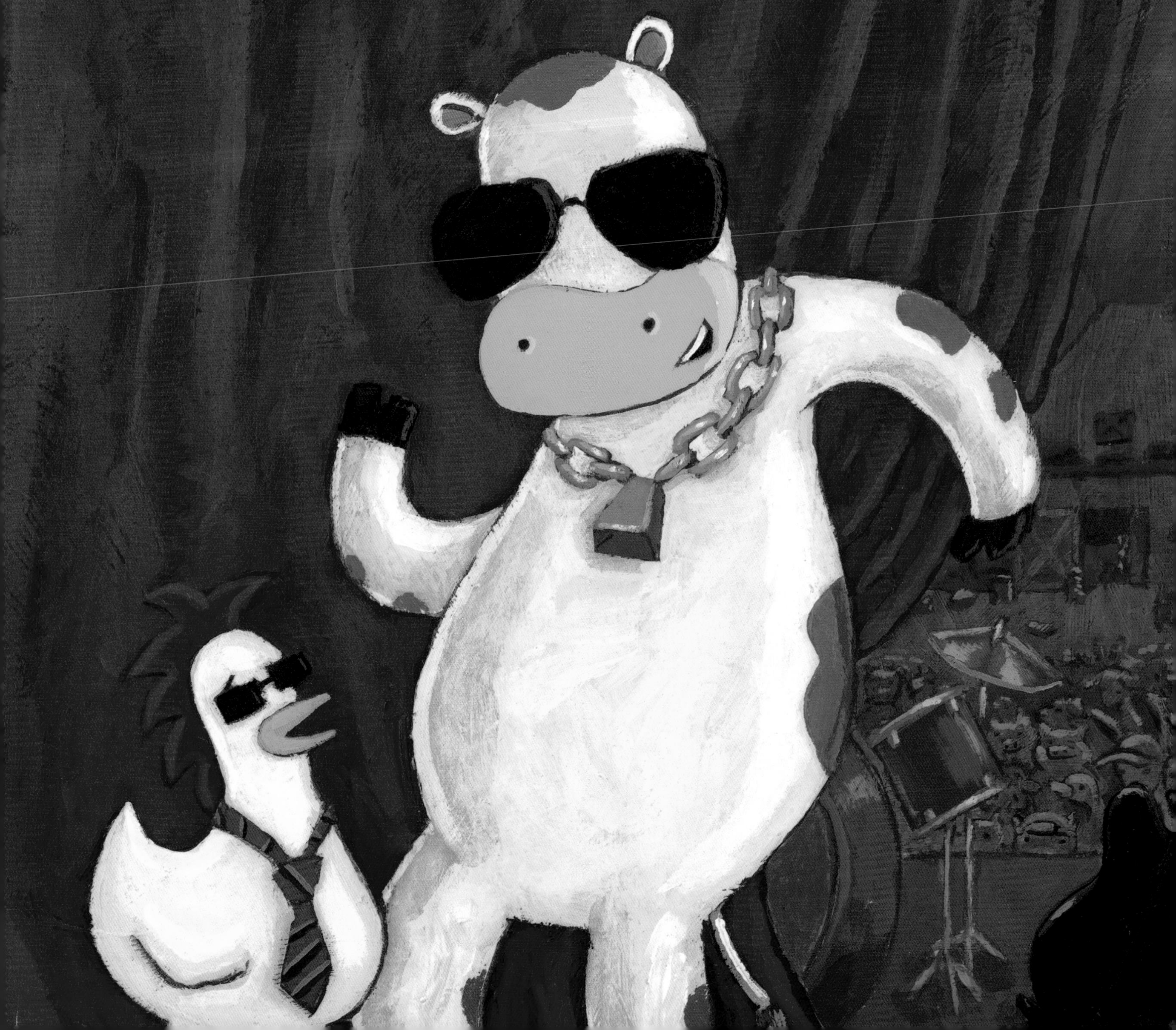

Sheep asks the crowd,

"Who's ready to rock?!"

and they go crazy!

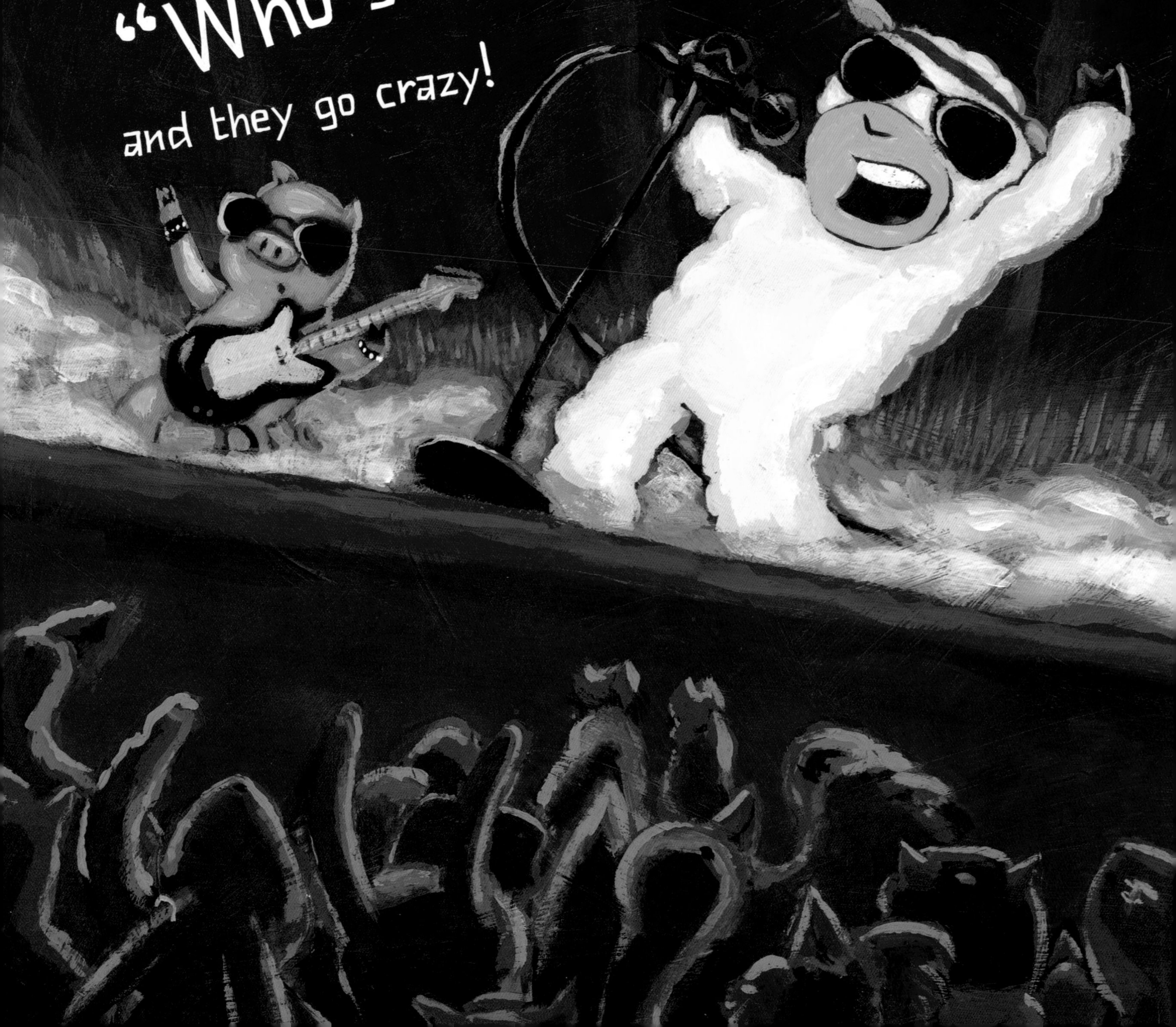

"1-2, 1-2-3-4!"

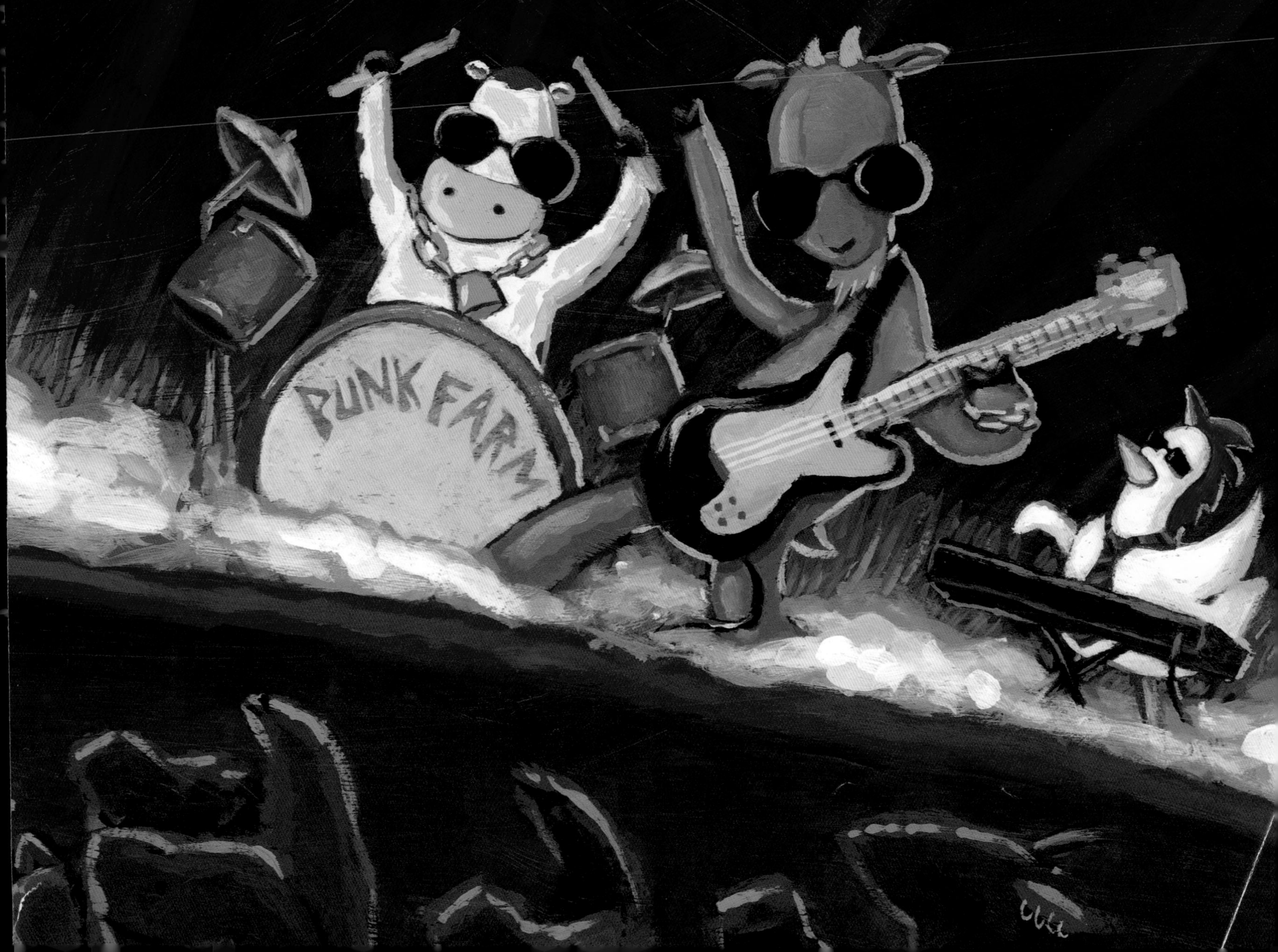
PUNK FARM

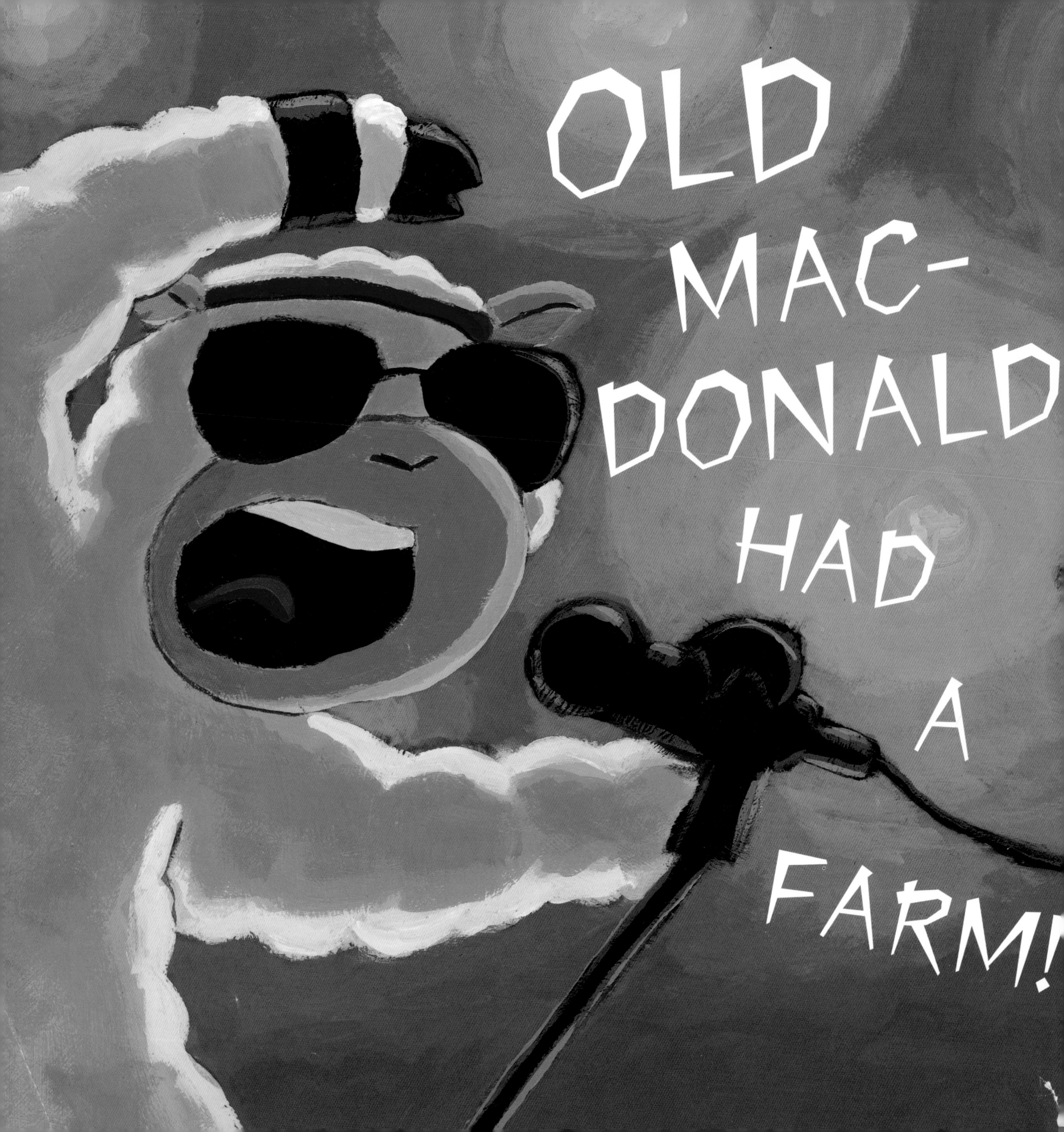
OLD MAC-DONALD HAD A FARM!

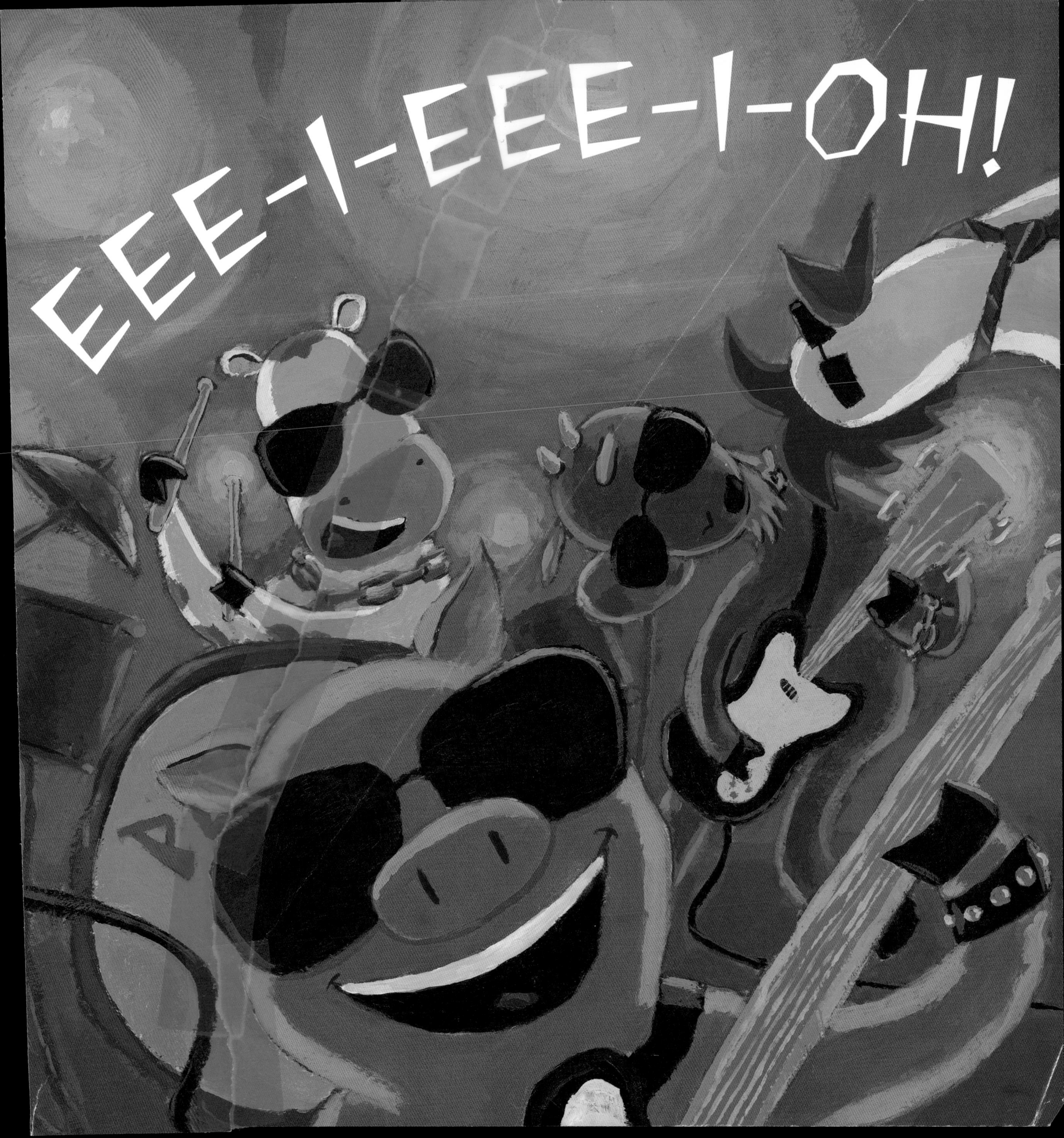
EEE-I-EEE-I-OH!

And on that farm he had a COW!

EEE-I-EEE-I-OH!

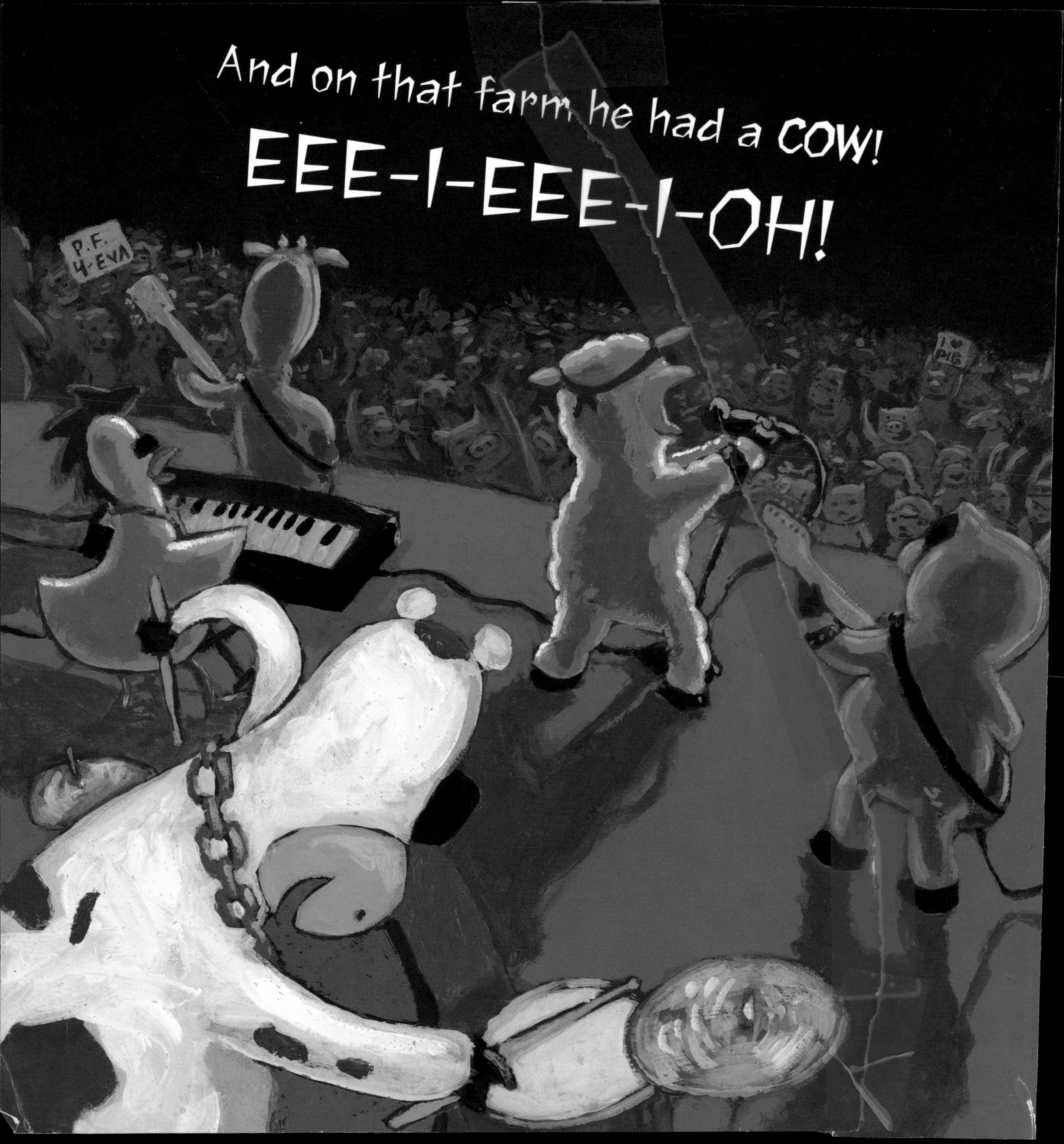
P.F.
4-EVA
I ♥ PIG

With a BOOM CRASH here
and a BOOM BOOM there.
Here a BOOM, there a CRASH,
everywhere a CRASH
CRASH!

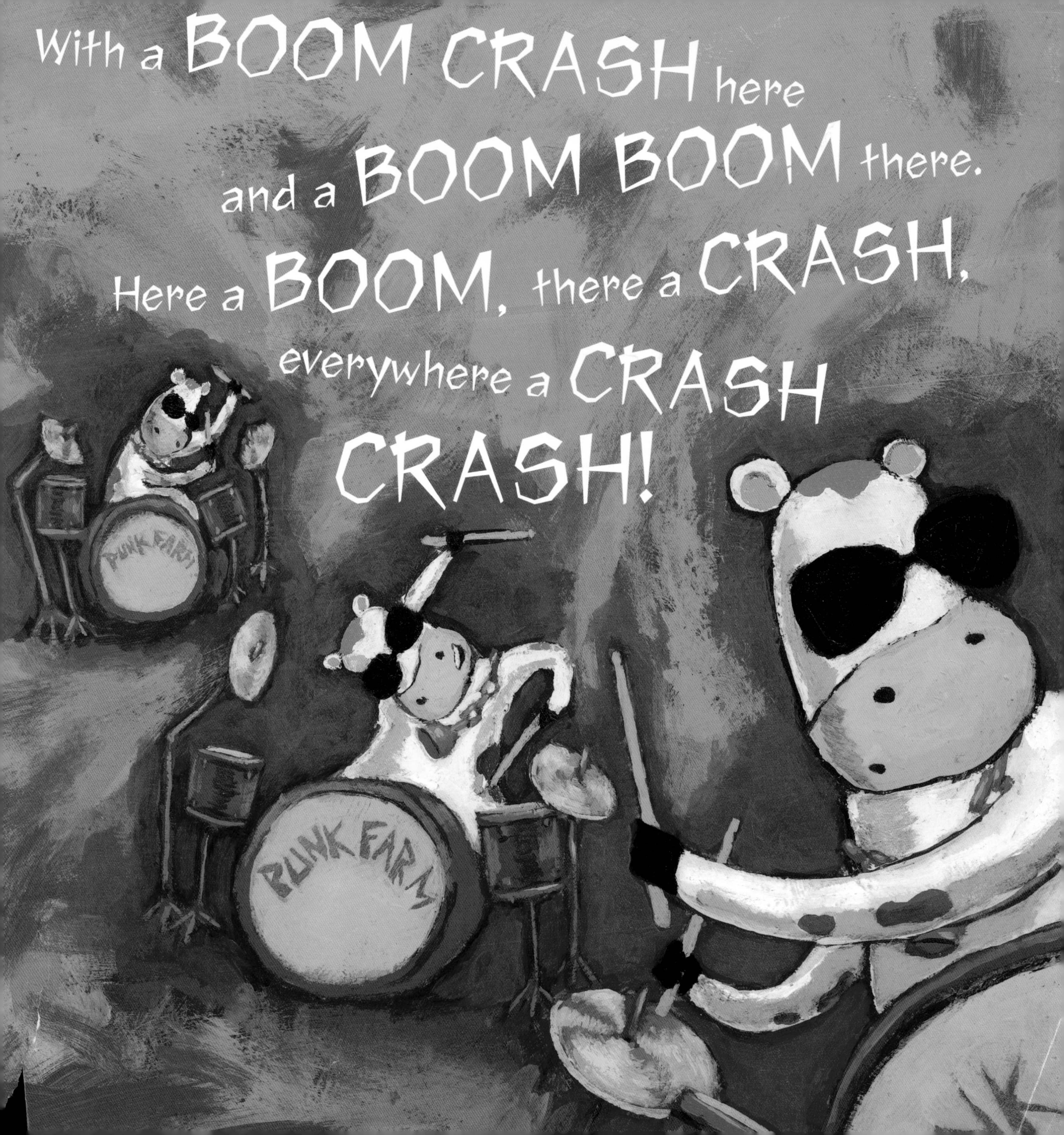
PUNK FARM
PUNK FARM

With a RAY ROO here
and a RAY REE there.
Here a REARRR,
there a ROOOOO,
everywhere a RAY
ROOOOO!

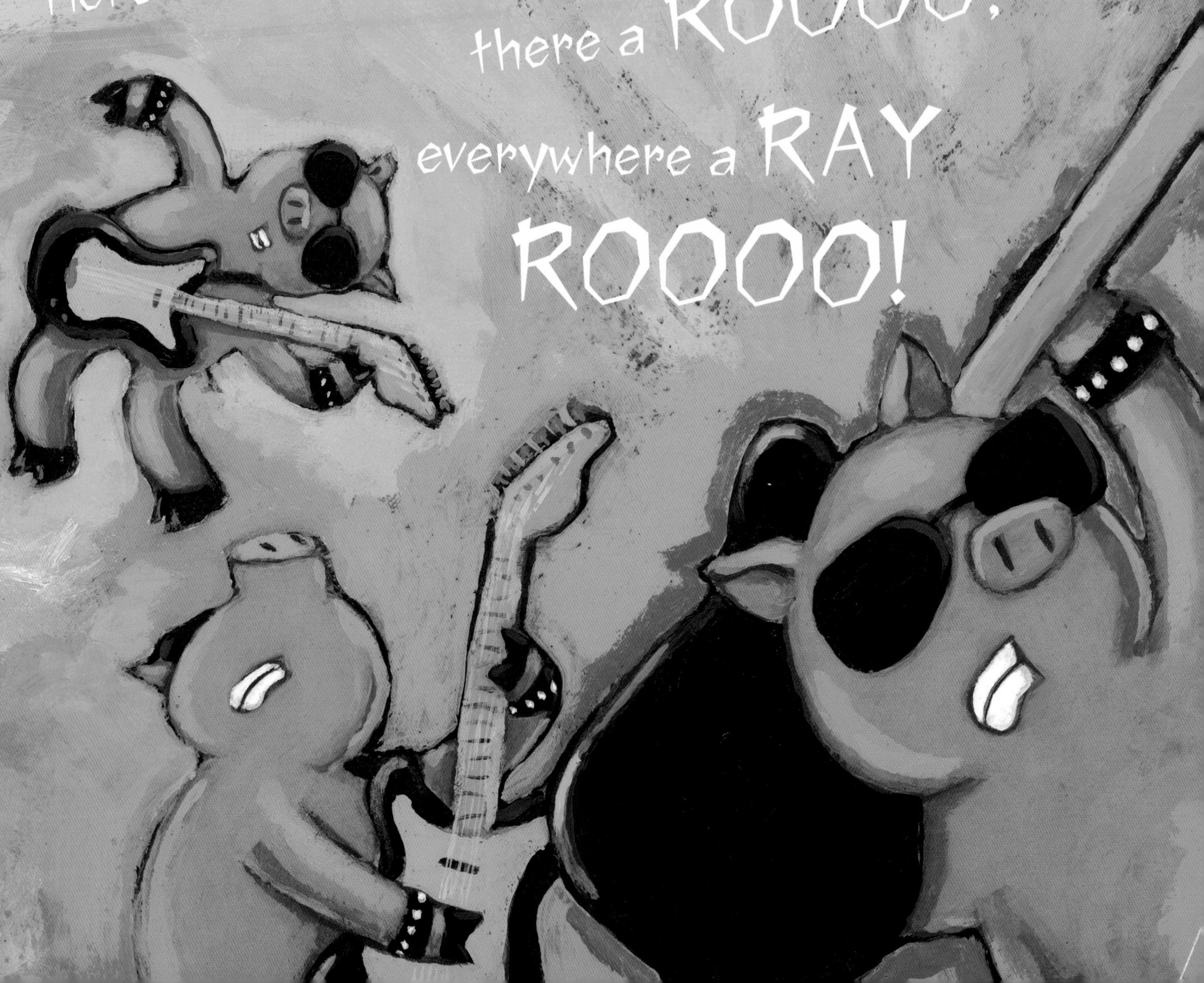

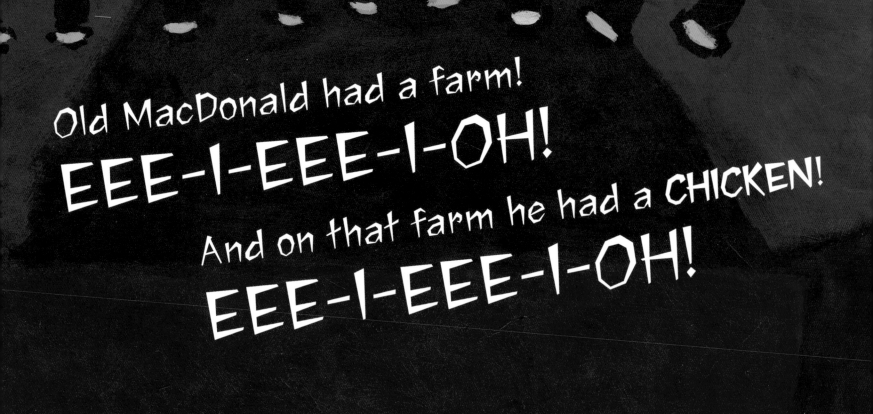

Old MacDonald had a farm!
EEE-I-EEE-I-OH!
And on that farm he had a CHICKEN!
EEE-I-EEE-I-OH!

With a BEEP BEEP here
and a BA BEEP there.
Here a BEEP, there a BEEP,
everywhere a
BEEP
BEEP!

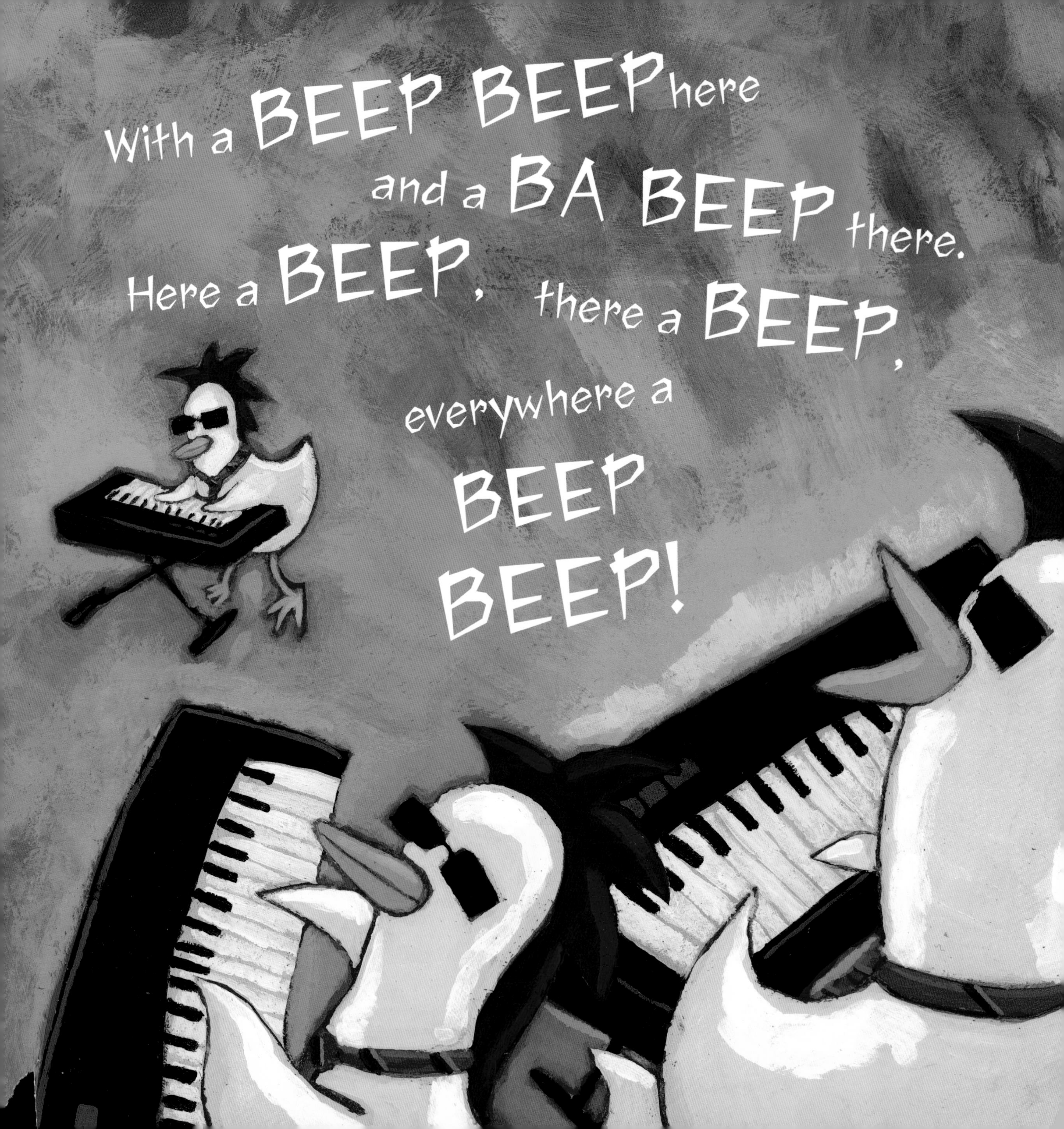

With a BRUM BRUM here
and a BA DUM there.
Here a BRUM, there a BRUM,
everywhere a BA
DUM!

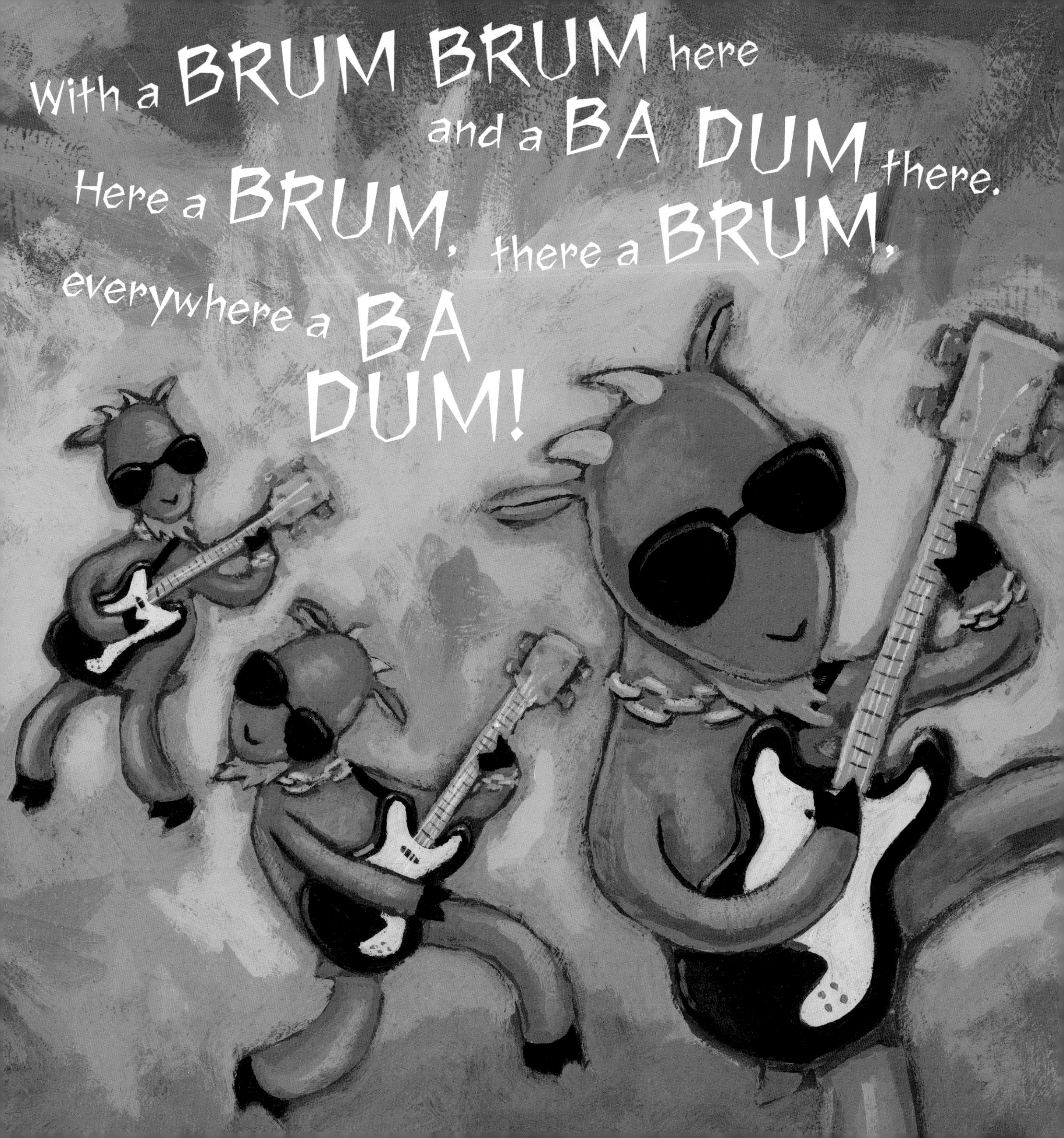

Punk Farm wails on their instruments one last time and delivers a blazing finale!

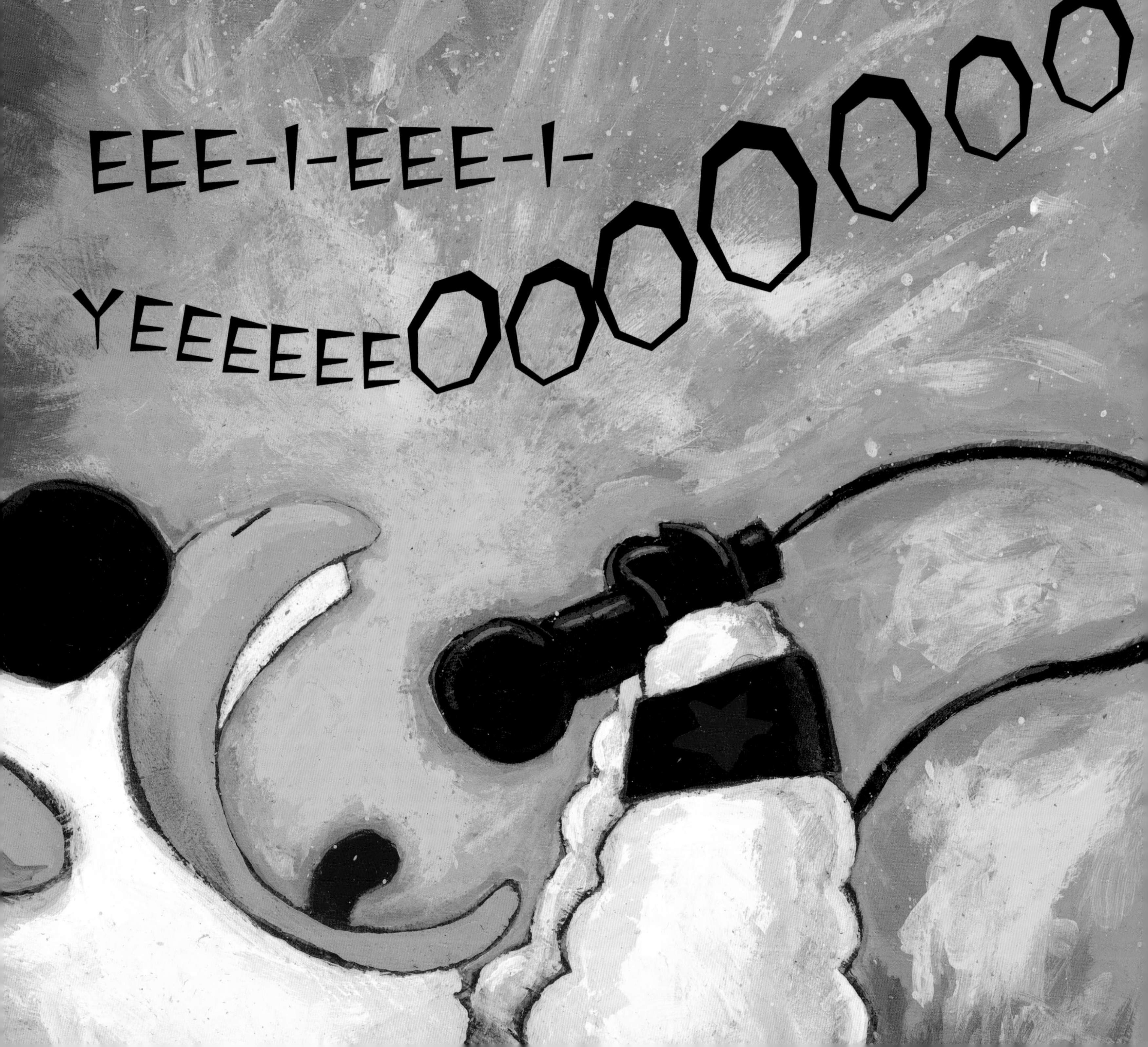
EEE-I-EEE-I-
YEEEEEEOOOOOOO

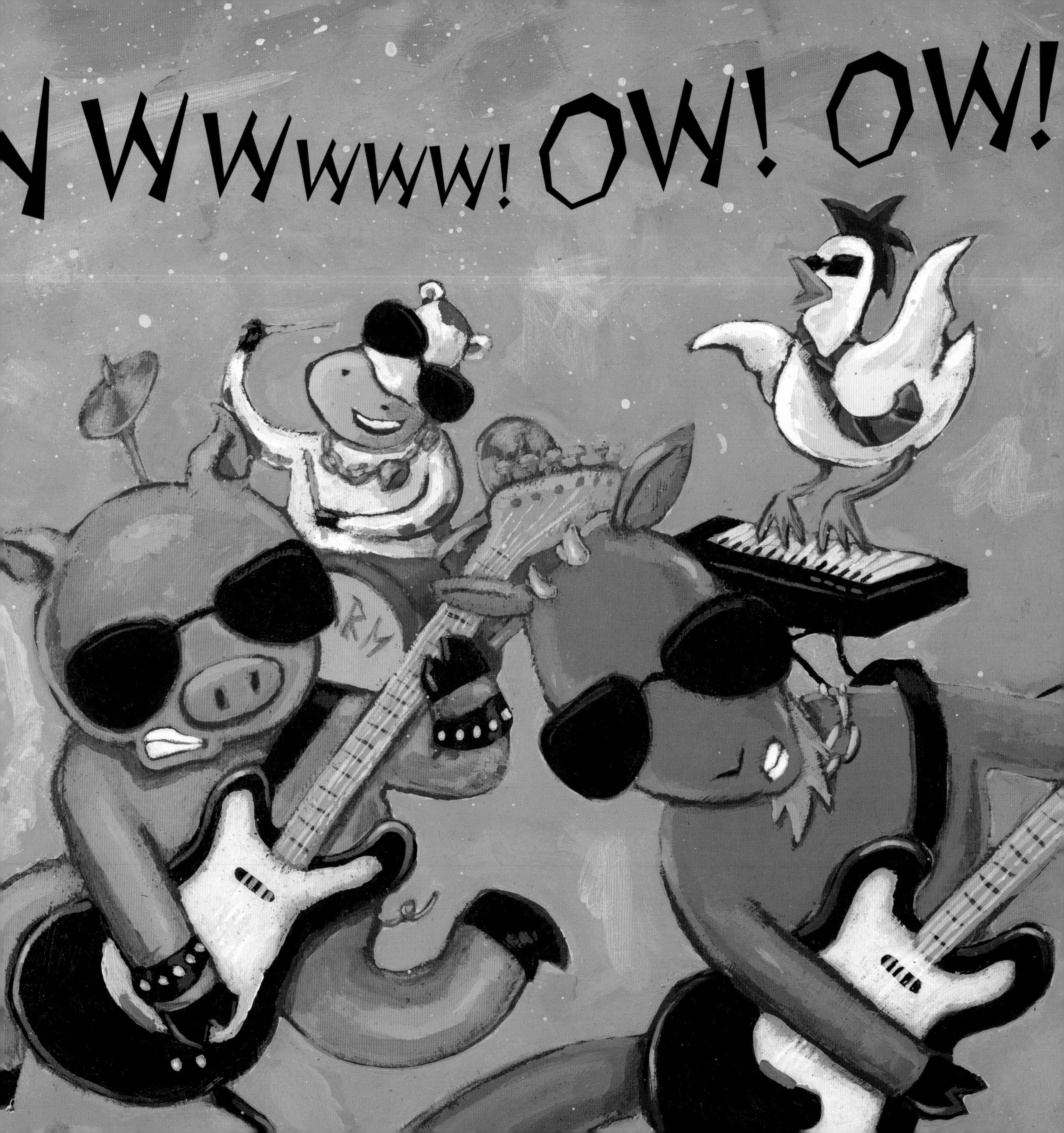
WWwww! OW! OW!

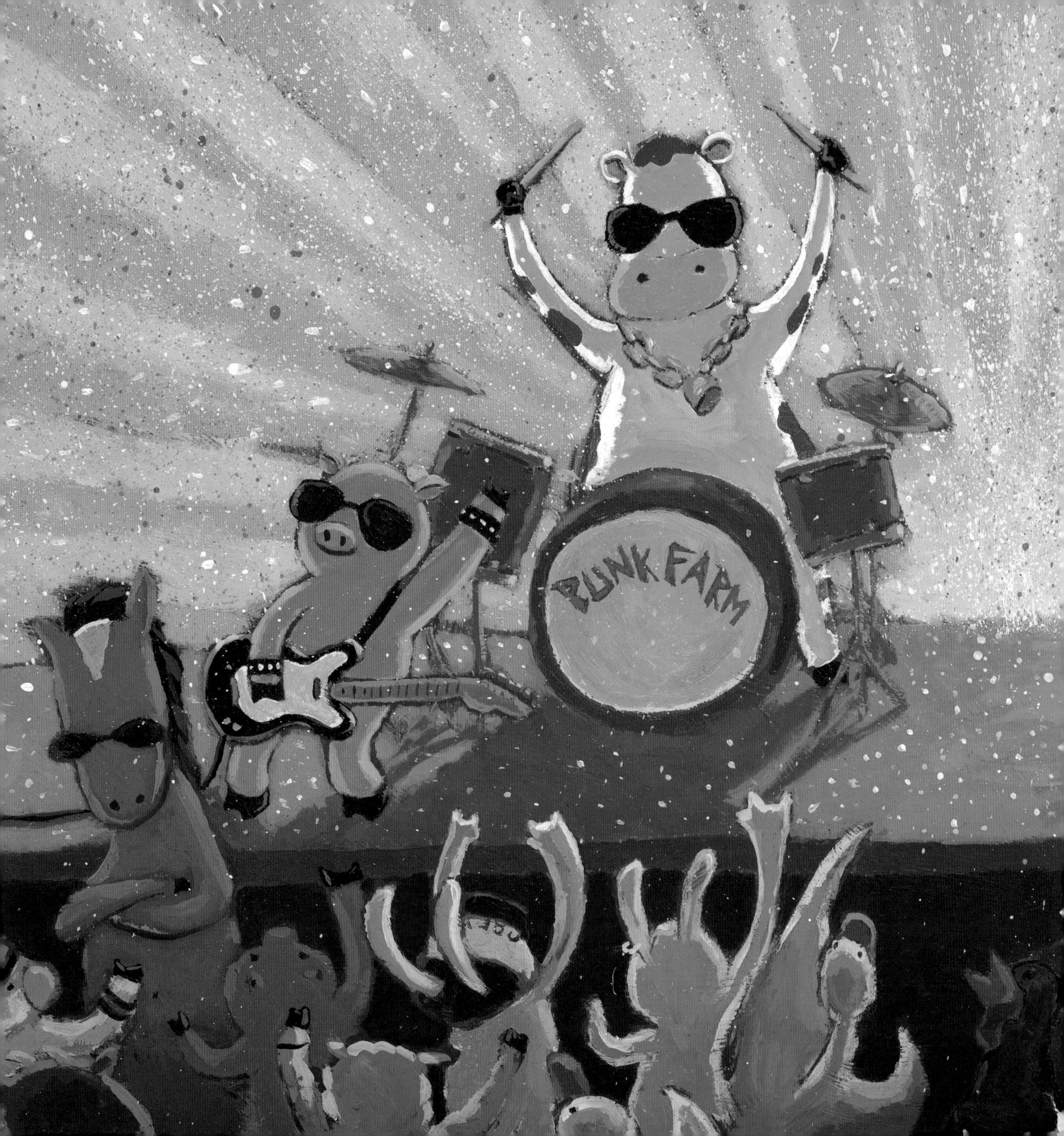
PUNK FARM

"Thank you, Wisconsin!"

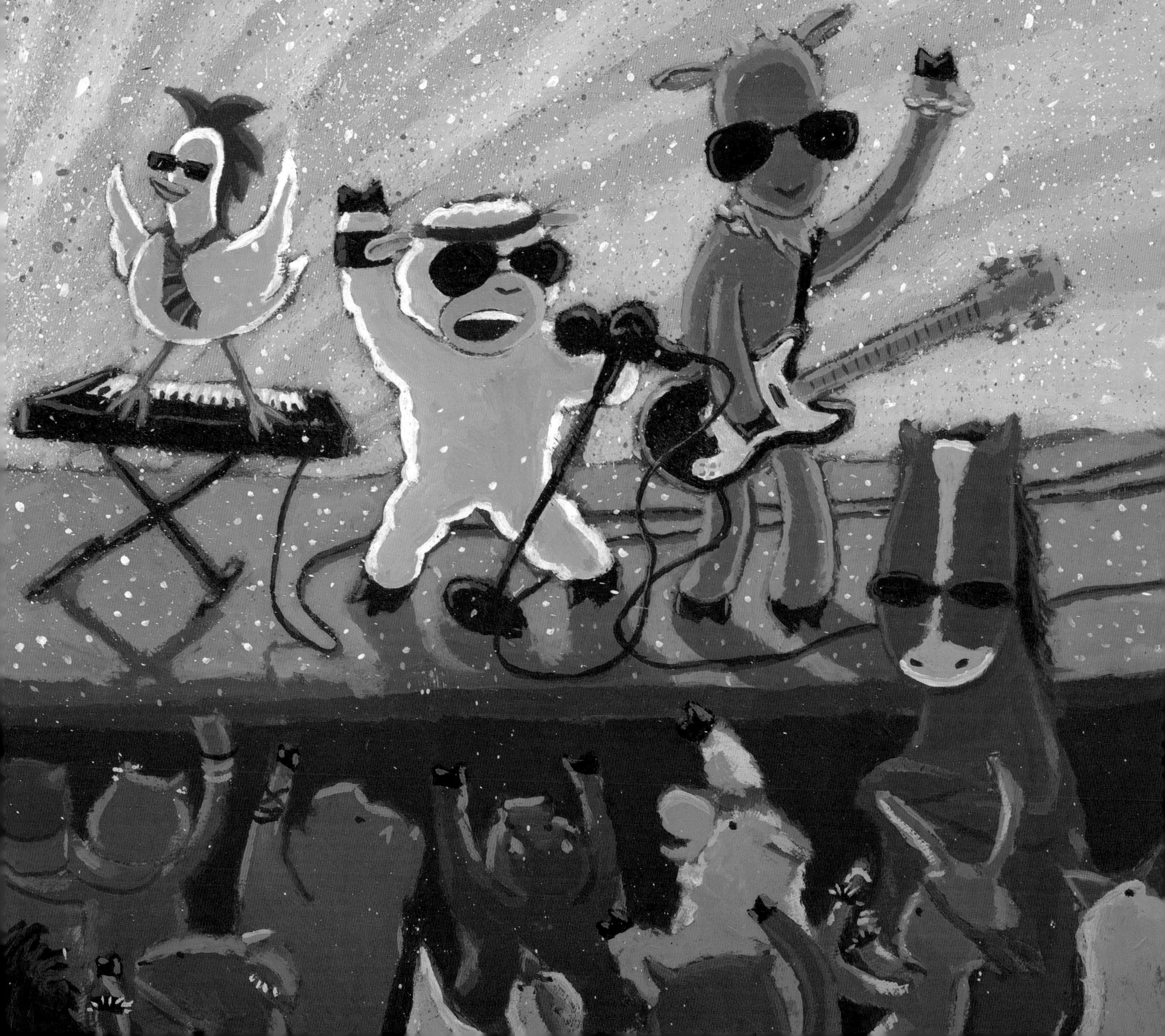

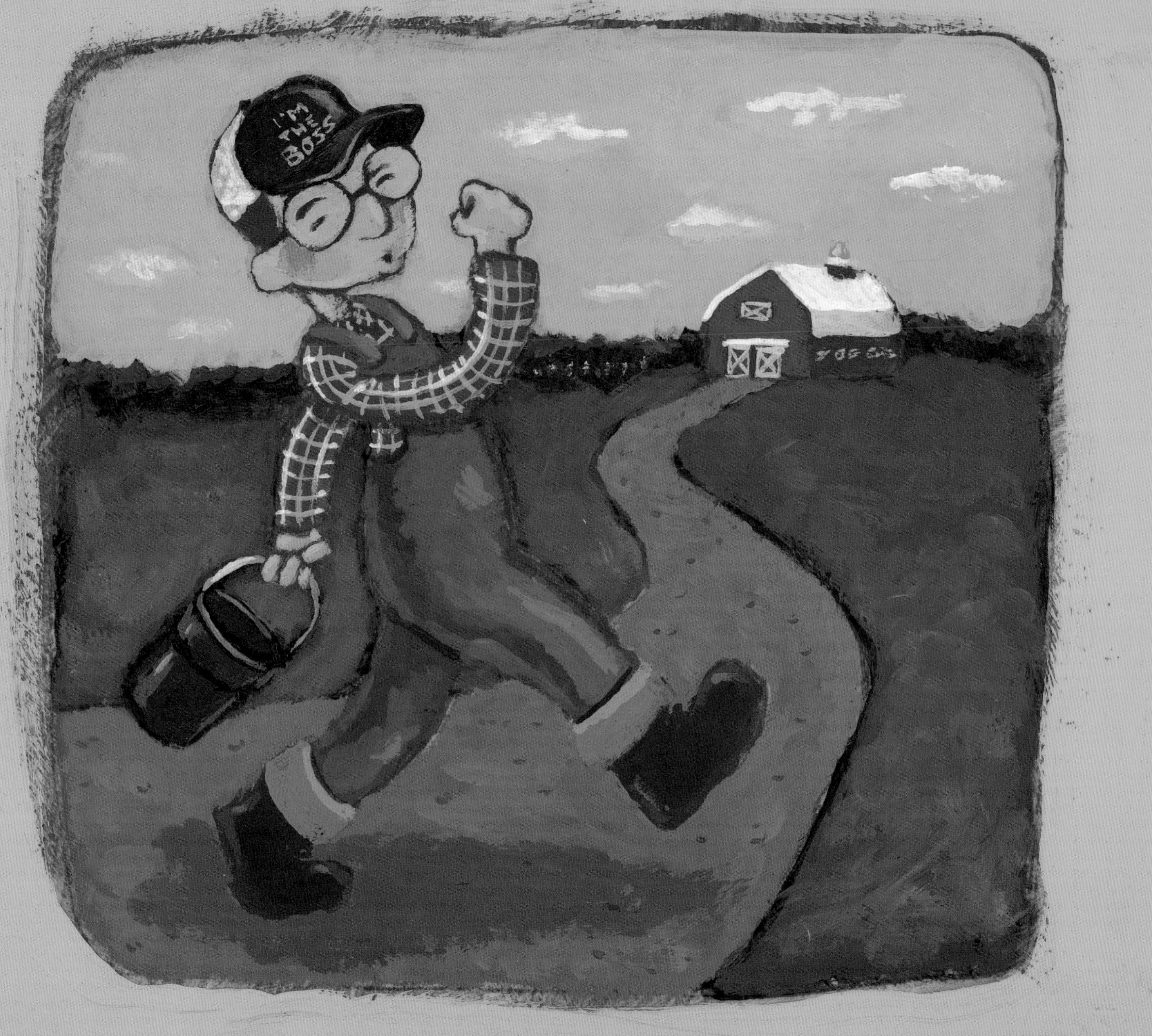
I'M THE BOSS

Soon the sun rises and so does Farmer Joe. He heads over to the barn for . . .

. . . a big day of work.

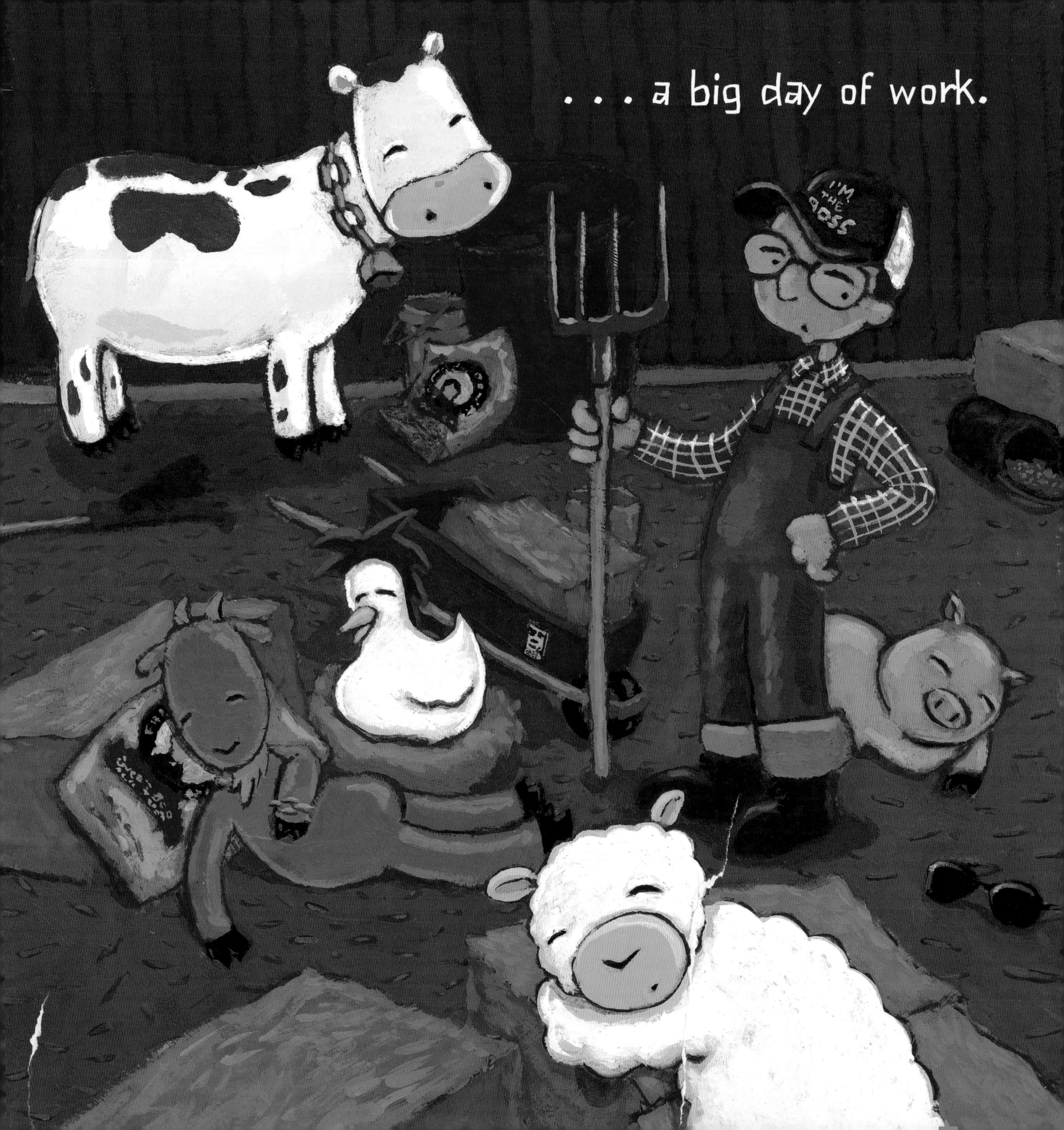

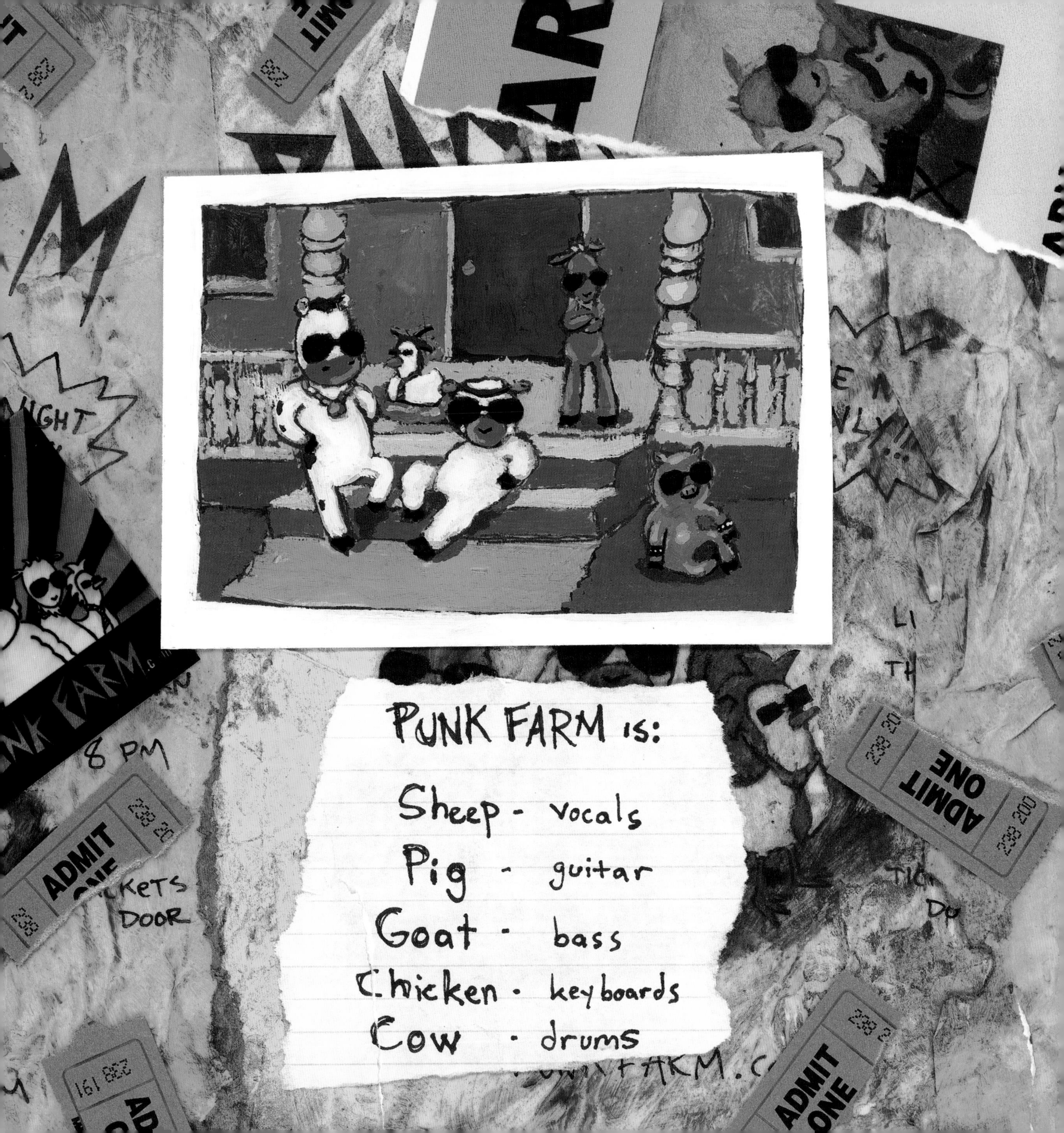
PUNK FARM is:
Sheep - vocals
Pig - guitar
Goat - bass
Chicken - keyboards
Cow - drums

WE'D LIKE TO THANK: OUR FAMILIES FOR BELIEVING IN US. THE HOLE IN THE WALL GANG FOR CONSTANTLY INSPIRING US. GREEN 15 AND THE LONDON STARS! THE HEROES OF THE TIME WARP KITCHEN! ALL OF OUR FRIENDS AT RANDOM. EVERYONE DOWN AT THE BARN. AND OF COURSE— FARMER JOE!

Peace + Rock
Forever,
PUNK FARM

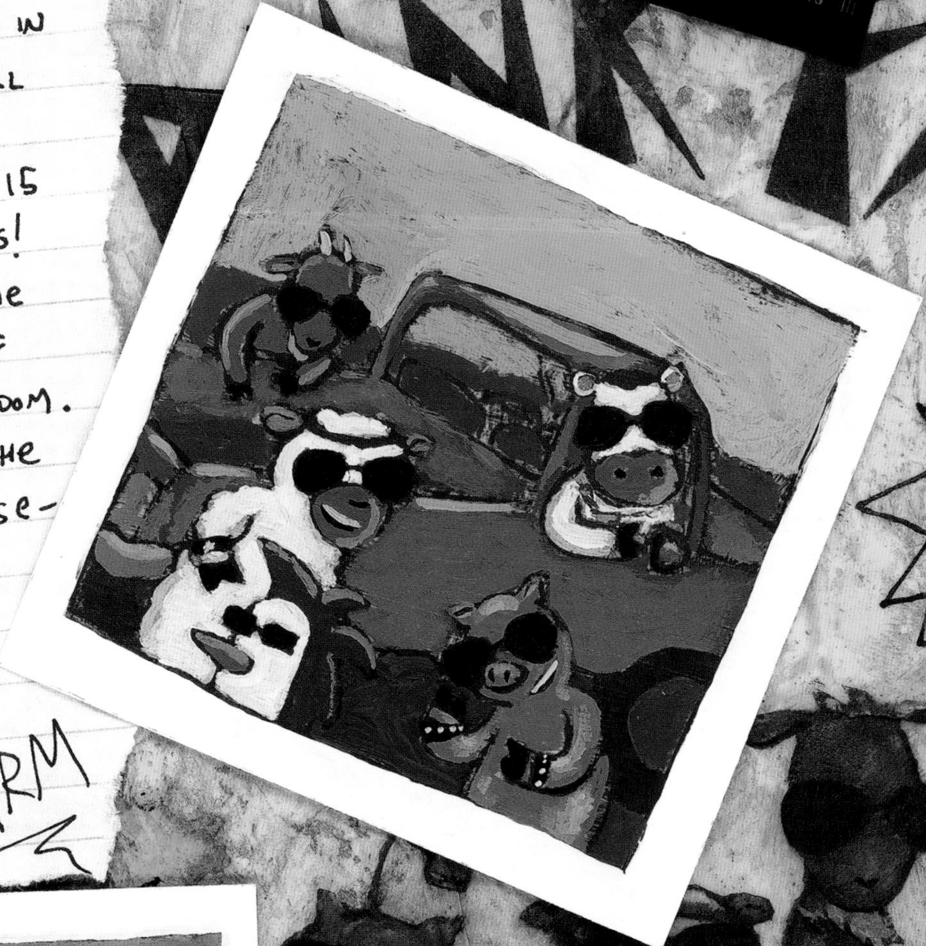

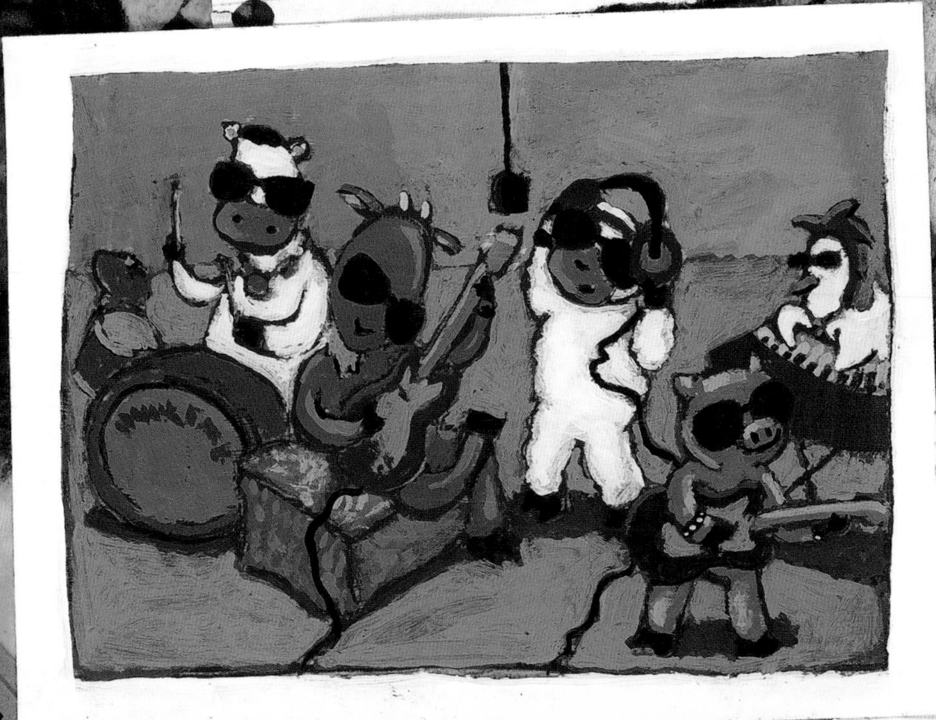

Old MacDonald had a f
EEE-I-EEE-I-OH!
and on that
EEE-